The Blue Rose Fairy Book by Maurice Baring

Maurice Baring OBE was born on 27th April 1874 in Mayfair, London. He was the fifth son of eight children to Edward Charles Baring, first Baron Revelstoke, of the Baring banking family, and his wife Louisa Emily Charlotte Bulteel.

After the obligatory years at Eton College he went to Trinity College, Cambridge.

His early career in the diplomatic service was cut short but it gave him a thirst for travel and he did so widely, particularly in Russia. During the Russo-Japanese war of 1904/5 he reported as an eye-witness for the London Morning Post.

In 1909 Baring, who thought of himself as agnostic, converted to Roman Catholicism. A decision which he stated was "the only action in my life which I am quite certain I have never regretted."

When the horror of World War I enveloped Europe in 1914 he enlisted with the Royal Flying Corps, and served as an assistant to David Henderson and Hugh Trenchard (the two responsible for establishing the RFC) on the Western Front in France.

In 1918, Baring served as a staff officer in the Royal Air Force and was appointed Officer of the Order of the British Empire in the 1918 Birthday Honours List.

With the end of the war came his development as a writer. Before the war his works had mainly centrered on journalism, short stories and poetry. Now Baring began to write novels.

In 1925 he gained an honorary commission as a wing commander in the Reserve of Air Force Officers. After his death, Trenchard was to write, "He was the most unselfish man I have ever met or am likely to meet. The Flying Corps owed to this man much more than they know or think."

The last decades of his life proved to be a descent into chronic health problems. For the final 15 years of his life he was debilitated by the increasing onset of Parkinson's Disease.

He was widely known socially, and especially frequented with some of the Cambridge Apostles (an intellectual society at the University founded in 1820), The Coterie (a fashionable group of aristocrats and intellectuals of the 1910s). Baring was staunch in his anti-intellectualism with respect to the arts, and often displayed a lighter side with his pranks on others.

"By all accounts, the real Baring was a charming, affable gentleman who knew how to laugh and had no fear of making a fool of himself."

Maurice Baring, dramatist, poet, novelist, translator, essayist, travel writer and war correspondent, died at Beaufort Castle on 14th December 1945 at the age of 71.

Index of Contents

THE GLASS MENDER

Once upon a time there lived a King and a Queen who had one daughter called Rainbow. When she was christened, the people of the city were gathered together outside the cathedral, and amongst them was an old gipsy woman. The gipsy wanted to go inside the cathedral, but the Beadle would not let her, because he said there was no room. When the ceremony was over, and the King and Queen walked out, followed by the Head Nurse who carried the baby, the gipsy called out to them:

"Your daughter will be very beautiful, and as happy as the day is long, until she sees the Spring!" And then she disappeared in the crowd.

The King and the Queen took counsel together and the King said: "That gipsy was evidently a fairy, and what she said bodes no good."

"Yes," said the Queen, "there is only one thing to be done: Rainbow must never see the Spring, nor even hear that there is such a thing."

So an order was issued to the whole city, that if any one should say the word "Spring" in the presence of Princess Rainbow he would have his head cut off. Moreover, it was settled that the Princess should never be allowed to go outside the palace, and during the springtime she should be kept entirely indoors.

The King and the Queen lived in a city which was on the top of a hill, and had a wall round it, and the King's palace was in the middle of it. In the springtime Rainbow was taken to a high tower which looked on to the little round city, and from her window you could see the spires of the churches, the ramparts, and the broad green plain beyond. But a curtain made of canvas was fastened outside Rainbow's window, so that she could see nothing, and she was not allowed to go outside her tower until the springtime was over.

Rainbow grew up into a most beautiful Princess, with grey eyes and fair hair, and until she was sixteen all went well, and nothing happened to interfere with her happiness.

It was on her sixteenth birthday, which was in April, and she was sitting alone in her room, looking at her birthday presents, when she began to wonder for the first time why she was shut up in her tower during three months of the year, and why a curtain was placed outside her window, so that she could see nothing outside. Her mother and her nurse had told her that this was done so that she might not fall ill, and she had always believed it; but on that day, for the first time, she began to wonder whether there might be any other reason as well. It was a lovely Spring day, and the sun shone through the canvas curtain which was stretched outside Rainbow's open window; a breeze came into her room from the outside world, and Rainbow felt a great longing to tear aside the curtain and to see what was happening out of doors.

At that very moment, a sound came into her room from the city: it was the sound of two or three notes played on some small reed or pipe, unlike those of any of the musical instruments she had heard in the palace, more tuneful and more artless and more gay. As she heard the few reedy notes of this little tune, she felt something which she had never known before. The whole room seemed to be full of a new sunshine, and she smelt the fragrance of the grass; she heard the blackbird whistling, and the lark singing; she saw the apple orchards in blossom, the violets peeping from under the leaves, the hedges covered with primroses, the daffodils fluttering in the wind, the fern uncrumpling her new leaves, the green slopes starred with crocuses; fields of buttercups and marigolds; forests paved with bluebells; lilac bushes; the trailing gold of the laburnums; and the sharp green of the awakening beech-trees; and she heard the cuckoo's note, and a thousand other unknown sounds of meadow, wood, and stream; and before her passed the whole pageant of the Spring, with its joyous music and its thousand and one sights.

The vision disappeared and she cried out: "Let me go into the world and let me taste and see this wonderful new thing!"

Rainbow said nothing about her vision, either to her parents or to her nurses, but she resolved to steal out of the palace as soon as she could, and to see in the world what her vision had shown her; but that very evening she fell ill, and she was obliged to go to bed. The next day she was no better, and a week passed and she was just as ill as ever. All the wisest physicians of the land examined her, but not one of them could say what was the matter with her; some of them prescribed medicines, and others strange things to eat and drink; but none of them did her the least good. The months went by, and Rainbow was still lying in bed, suffering from a strange malady which nobody could even find a name for. When the Spring was past, Rainbow was borne on a couch into the garden of the palace; but she got no better.

At last the Queen sent for a Wise Woman who lived in a wood near the city, and asked her advice. The Wise Woman was told Rainbow's history and what the gipsy had said, and after she had looked at Rainbow and spoken to her, she said to the Queen:

"I understand quite well what has happened. Your daughter has seen the Spring."

"But that's impossible," said the Queen, "for during the whole of the Spring months she has never left her room."

"Somehow or other the Spring has reached her," said the old woman, and then she asked Rainbow some more questions, and the end of this was that Rainbow told her about the tune she had heard on her birthday, and the vision she had seen.

"I knew it," said the old woman, "she heard somebody playing the Spring's own tune, and she won't get well until she hears it again, and even then her troubles will be far from ended." So saying the old woman went away.

The King at once sent for the court musicians and told them to play the Spring's Song. They fiddled, and they blew upon every kind of pipe and flute; they beat the cymbals and struck the harp; but none of these tunes kindled the slightest interest in Rainbow or roused her from her listlessness. The King then issued a proclamation saying that whoever should play the song that cured Rainbow would receive any reward he should ask for, and even, if he wished it, his daughter's hand.

The news was spread far and wide, and people came from the four corners of the world to play to the Princess.

First of all a lad came from the northern country, where he had slain a huge dragon in single combat, and he said that if any one knew the Song of Spring he did, for the birds themselves had taught it him; and when he was shown into the Princess's room he blew a blast on his horn, so strong that the rafters trembled, and so sweet that the palace seemed to be full of the scent of the northern forests. But Rainbow paid no heed, and the lad went his way.

Then an uncouth minstrel came from Greece; he had furry ears and a pointed beard, and he played on a double pipe and he said: "I know the Song of Spring if any one knows it, for the bees taught it me." He breathed on his pipe and the whole room seemed to be full of the smell of thyme, the murmur of reeds, and the drone of bees. But Rainbow paid no heed to him, and the uncouth minstrel went his way.

Then there came a man who carried a lyre. His face was beautiful and sad, and he said: "I know the Song of Spring if any one knows it, for I heard it played in the happy fields." And he struck his lyre and sang a song which was so lovely and so plaintive that the horses neighed in their stalls, the dogs came to listen, and the trees of the garden bent over the palace windows, and the King and the Queen and all the courtiers wept: but Rainbow paid no heed, and the man with the lyre went his way.

Then came a knight from over the sea, from the West Country; and he was the most splendid knight ever seen, and he carried neither harp nor pipe, and he said: "I know the Song of Spring if any one knows it, for I learnt it in the forests of Tintagel:" and he sang the song that only those who dwell in the forests of the West know, and it was a song of love. But Rainbow paid no heed, and the knight went his way.

Then Prince Charming came from the Golden Isles and said: "I know the Song of Spring if any one knows it, for my fairy-godmother gave me a flute, and when I play on it the elves dance round me in a ring": and he played a tune on his flute, and the lights and rainbows of the golden islands seemed to twinkle in the room. But Rainbow paid no heed, so Prince Charming went his way.

Then there came a Prince who was a changeling and who had been brought up in Fairyland itself, and he said: "I know the Song of Spring if any one knows it, for Proserpine, the Queen of the Fairies, herself taught me the song she heard in the Vales of Enna, when she was picking flowers in the Spring." And he sang of the Sicilian fields, a song of the swallow and the corn; and the song was like a vision, and the room seemed to be full of the sound of the southern seas; but Rainbow paid no heed, and the changeling went his way.

Then Prince Apollo himself came from Italy with his fiddle, and he said: "If I do not know the Song of Spring, who can know it? For my music excels that of all mortal men."

Prince Apollo struck up a tune on his fiddle and the room was filled with a glory; but Rainbow paid no heed, and Prince Apollo went away in a rage, saying that the Princess had no ear.

After this people gave up the quest, for they said: "If all these great people fail, how should we succeed?" Now it happened one day, when the springtime came round again, that two tumblers were playing at ball in the Princess's room to try and amuse her, and one of them in throwing, threw the ball and broke the pane of her casement; so a glass mender was sent for to mend the window, and there happened to be one that day just outside the palace.

The glass mender was a youth, and his eyes were blue and his cheeks fresh, and as he strode up the staircase to the Princess's room, he whistled on a small glass pipe the tune that glass menders have always whistled ever since the beginning of the world. Directly Rainbow heard this sound, she leaped from her bed and cried out:

"That is it! I hear it, the Song of Spring!" And as the glass mender came into the room with his basket and his tools, she said: "At last you've come! You've cured me, and I am now quite well again."

There was no doubt about it. Rainbow from that moment was cured, and the glass mender went to the King and claimed his reward.

At first the King was vexed that his daughter should have to wed a humble glass mender, but he did not dare play any tricks with his daughter's life after what had happened, for fear she should fall ill again; and besides, Rainbow was determined to marry him, and as he was so young, so handsome, and so well-spoken, the King told the Queen that he was very likely a Prince in disguise.

But the glass mender made two conditions about his marriage: the first was that he was to continue to be a wandering glass mender who earned his living by going from city to city, and from village to village, mending glass, and the second was that Rainbow was never to ask him where he came from nor who were his parents, and that she should call him Blue Eyes, nor ever ask him whether he had another name.

This convinced the King that Blue Eyes was a Prince in disguise, and the conditions were readily agreed to, and Rainbow and Blue Eyes were married without further delay. The King gave them each a white pony for a wedding present and they started off on their travels.

They rode through the fields and the woods, from village to village, sleeping now in a house and now out of doors, and for the first time in her life Rainbow tasted and saw the Spring; and no words can tell how happy they were: all day long Blue Eyes played a tune on his glass pipe, and he showed Rainbow the haunts of the birds and the beasts; and whenever they came to a village it was as though they brought the sunshine of the morning with them, for as soon as any one looked at Blue Eyes, they could not help being happy, and when he played on his pipe people danced for joy. They wandered over the wide world, and they saw every kind of country and city, and wherever they went smiling faces met them and they made sad people happy, and happy people happier still.

When they were in the woods or meadows the birds and beasts seemed to know Blue Eyes, and he talked with them just as if they were real people; and the most savage beasts—wolves and bears and wild boars—were as tame as lap-dogs when he spoke to them; and the nightingales used to perch on Blue Eyes' shoulder in the evening, and sing, as he rode with Rainbow through the forest; the bees and butterflies used to fly in front of them and show them the way.

The years went by and they had a little son who was called Blue Boy, who grew up just like his father, and talked with the birds and beasts directly he could speak, and they were all three of them together as happy as the day is long.

One Spring evening they arrived rather late in a wood, and after they had made a fire and cooked their supper, Rainbow and Blue Boy went to sleep, and Blue Eyes sat by the fire for he said he wasn't sleepy.

After Rainbow had been sleeping for a few hours she woke up with a start. The moon had risen and the camp-fire had not yet gone out, but the ashes were smouldering and there by the fire sat Blue Eyes. Rainbow could see him distinctly, but he seemed to her to look different from usual; strange, beautiful, and more like a fairy Prince than a glass mender. Sitting with him by the fire was a lovely maiden with roses in her hair and some ears of wheat in her hand, and a silver sickle hanging from her girdle. They were talking together. Rainbow was so surprised that she uttered a cry, and immediately the beautiful maiden vanished into the wood. Blue Eyes at once went to Rainbow, but she turned over on her side and pretended to be asleep.

The next day Blue Eyes said nothing about the strange maiden, and Rainbow began to be jealous and sad. She tried not to think of it, but she could not get rid of the thought that perhaps Blue Eyes loved somebody else. The next evening they again camped out in the wood, and Rainbow said she was tired and lay down to sleep early; but she only pretended to go to sleep, and she was really wide awake.

As soon as Blue Eyes thought that Rainbow was asleep, he blew a note on his glass pipe, and once more the strange maiden came out of the wood, and she and Blue Eyes talked together in a whisper, and once more Blue Eyes seemed to look quite different, and not at all like a glass mender, only, as it was dark that night, Rainbow could not see him distinctly.

The next morning Blue Eyes again said nothing about the strange maiden, and Rainbow was sadder than ever. If Blue Eyes would only explain, she said to herself, everything would be all right. So as they were riding through the wood, Rainbow said to him:

"I saw you in the wood last night talking to a strange maiden; and, Blue Eyes, you looked different. I am sure now that you are not a glass mender; and now that I have seen you talking to that strange maiden, I shall have no peace until you tell me who you are and who she is."

"Alas, alas, alas!" said Blue Eyes. "Oh; Rainbow, why could you not trust me? I must tell you now, whether I wish it or no, but you have destroyed our happiness, and I shall have to leave you. My name is Spring, and I was talking to my sister Summer; and now I shall have to leave you, for I can only take a mortal shape as long as nobody knows who I am."

Then Rainbow wept bitterly, and said:

"Do you mean you must leave me for ever, and that I shall never see you again?"

"There is one hope left," said Blue Eyes. "We shall meet again if you are able to find me. You will have to search all over the world, and you will not find me until you recognise my look and my voice in the speech or the look of a human being; and if you fail to recognise it, when it is there, you will never find me at all."

"And when I recognise you either in the speech or the look of a human being," said Rainbow, "what must I do then?"

"Then," said Blue Eyes, "you must say this:

'Blue Eyes, Blue Eyes, come back to me,
Over the hills and over the sea;
Brother of Summer, husband and friend,
Come and stay till the world shall end.'"

"But what will happen," asked Rainbow, "if I make a mistake and say the rhyme to some one who seems to have your look and your speech, when really they are not there?"

"If you make a mistake," said Blue Eyes, "you will never see me again."

Rainbow again began to weep bitterly. She implored Blue Eyes to forgive her, but she no longer begged him to stay, for she knew it was useless; and Blue Eyes kissed her and Blue Boy, and when he had said good-bye, he leapt on to his pony and galloped off into the wood. As he galloped away his appearance changed; his glass mender's clothes fell away from him; instead of his blue cap, there was a crown of dew on his head, and he was clothed with the petals of snowdrops and cowslips; he wore a rainbow for a scarf, which fluttered in the wind; his pony changed into a white horse with silver wings; in his hand he carried a large wand of almond blossom, and a starling perched on his wrist. And as he galloped through the wood, the hoofs of his steed left behind them a trail of twinkling anemones. Thus he galloped on until he disappeared into the heart of the forest, and Rainbow was left alone with Blue Boy.

After she had had a long cry she dried her eyes and began at once to look for Blue Eyes. She wandered on through the wood with Blue Boy until they came to a hermit's cave. The hermit lived there all the year round, and his only companions were the birds and the beasts of the forest, and Rainbow thought if she talked to him she would perhaps hear the voice or see the look of Blue Eyes. But when she spoke to him she saw that he had forgotten what human beings were like, and he gave Rainbow and Blue Boy some bread and milk just as though they were birds. Then he opened his big book and began reading in it, and no longer noticed their presence.

The months went by, and Rainbow searched everywhere. She searched all through the summer, and although she met many kind faces, and saw many a happy smile, and heard many a young voice, nowhere did she meet any one who in the least reminded her of Blue Eyes.

When the winter came, they went to a city, and Blue Boy, who was growing up into a big boy, was apprenticed to a glass mender, and Rainbow and he lived together in a little room in the glass mender's house. The glass mender had a pretty daughter called Joan, and she had a tame blackbird which she kept in a wicker cage. All through the winter the city had been muffled in snow, and it had been bitterly cold; at last the snow melted; and March came with his boisterous wind and his cold showers of sleet and rain.

But one day the rain stopped; the sun shone in the blue sky, and Joan cried out:

"This is the first Spring day!" She ran out of doors with her bird cage and hung it up on the wall outside the house, and although there were as yet no green leaves anywhere, the blackbird knew that the spring had come, and he began to sing. While Joan was looking at the blackbird, Rainbow was watching her from her window, and was thinking to herself. "Surely now I shall hear the voice of Blue Eyes or see his look!" She was on the point of calling out:

"Blue Eyes, Blue Eyes, come back to me,"

when Joan looked up at her and met her gaze; and laughed, and blushed, and ran away. Rainbow knew that it was neither the voice nor the look of Blue Eyes; and she cried from disappointment.

By the time the spring was over, Blue Boy had learned his trade, and he was able to work on his own account and to support his mother, so they left the city together when the summer came, and they went from village to village and from city to city, mending broken window panes.

The years went by. Blue Boy was almost a man, and still Rainbow had not come across any one who had reminded her of Blue Eyes. She was sad, because she knew that in a year's time Blue Boy would be a man, and that it would be time for him to marry, and that she would then be left all alone. She knew that this was the last year that she and Blue Boy would be together.

One day they were walking through a grassy wood which was yellow with cowslips. It was a lovely April morning, and in the wood a lot of children were playing, and making chains and wreaths with the cowslips.

"Now, at last," thought Rainbow, "I shall hear the voice of Blue Eyes." She ran up to the children, but when the children saw her running towards them, they were frightened, and they ran away into the wood, and although she called and called they would not come back.

A little further on they came to a lovely village on a hill, overlooking a river which was a small arm of the sea. The hill was covered with orchards which were in full blossom, and in front of the little white straw-thatched cottages the neat flower-beds were full of sweet-smelling violets.

Rainbow and Blue Boy stayed in this village, and found plenty of work. One evening Rainbow was strolling in a lane on the top of the hill; the steep lane had on each side of it two grassy banks, on the top of which bushes and brambles and nut-trees grew so thickly that the ends of their boughs almost met across the lane, and the banks were covered with primroses. Walking along this lane, with their faces towards the sunset, Rainbow met a youth and a maiden; they were whispering to each other little broken words, with many sighs and smiles, and their talk was like the talk of two birds.

Rainbow's heart leapt as she heard them, and she was just going to cry out:

"Blue Eyes, Blue Eyes, come back to me,"

when they caught sight of her and stopped talking, and Rainbow knew that Blue Eyes was not there.

Then came the month of May, and the woods grew green and the lilac blossomed, and Rainbow grew sadder and sadder. One night she could not sleep, and she got up and walked through the moonlit village, right down to the quay by the river-side where the fishermen kept their boats and their nets. Many of the fishermen were out fishing on the sea, and one of them, a young lad, was setting the brown sail of his boat on the river, and as he did so, he sang a song which was like this:

"I have a cottage I love well,
In the sweet west countree:
And there my love and I shall dwell,
When I come back from sea.

We'll stow the sail and stow the oar,
And oh, how glad she'll be
To mend the nets upon the shore,
When I come back from sea.

I have a cottage on the hill,
Just right for her and me,
And she will say 'I love you still,'
When I come back from sea."

The fisherman's voice was so glad and joyous as he sang this song, that Rainbow thought Blue Eyes must be there, and she ran to the shore. At that moment the moonlight fell full upon the fisherman, so that Rainbow could see his face, and she stopped herself calling out just in time, for she saw he was not at all like Blue Eyes.

During that same month Blue Boy fell in love with a Dairy Maid called Cherry-Ripe, and it was arranged that they should be married at Michaelmas. But as Michaelmas drew near, Rainbow grew sadder and sadder, because she could not bear to think what she would do without Blue Boy.

September came, and the corn was carried, and the leaves began to turn gold. On Michaelmas Eve, Rainbow was sitting in her garden watching the autumn sunset. Not far from her garden, which was on the side of a steep hill, there was a quarry in which there was an old seat, and this was a favourite spot for lovers, for from this place you could see the little river, all the village and the sea beyond, and the view was beautiful. Rainbow thought she would walk to the quarry, so as to get a better view of the sunset.

When she got there, she saw an old couple sitting on the seat. The man was a fisherman; his face was bronzed and wrinkled by the wind and the waves, and the woman's hair was grey and silvery. They did not notice Rainbow coming, and the old woman said to the man:

"Do you remember how we used to meet here in the days when you were courting me?"

And the old man said: "It was in the spring, and the apple-trees were out."

And the old woman said: "Ah! I was a comely lass then. There was no one like me in the village. Folks wouldn't believe it now, what with my white hair and my wrinkles."

And the old man said: "I see no difference in you, lassie. You've the same lovely blue eyes as you always had, and if your hair has turned silver, it's none the less fair for that."

And the old woman said: "And I see no difference in you, Sweetheart; you're just as strong and as brave as ever."

And the old man said: "Why, it's forty years ago, but it makes nought to us, for as long as I've got you, and you've got me, we shan't see any change in each other, for with us it has always been springtide and courting time, and it always will be."

And the old man looked at the old woman, and smiled and took her hand, and her eyes filled with tears. And when Rainbow saw this, before she knew what happened, she had called out:

"Blue Eyes, Blue Eyes, come back to me,
Over the hills and over the sea.
Brother of Summer, husband and friend,
Come and stay till the world shall end."

As soon as she had said this, Blue Eyes stood before her just as he had been when he rode away, clothed in snowdrops and cowslips, wearing the rainbow for a scarf, and carrying a branch of blossom in his hand.

Rainbow was so glad to see Blue Eyes that she almost fainted. She led him to her cottage, and there she wept a long time for joy. Then Blue Eyes told her that he would never leave her again, but that he could not live on the earth a second time in the guise of a glass mender. During the spring they would ride through the world, scattering sunshine, laughter, and hope; mortals would see them, but they would not know who they were. During the summer and the autumn they would be invisible to mortals, and during the winter they would slumber in the Diamond Palace of his mother, the Snow Queen.

They waited to see Blue Boy and Cherry-Ripe married, and Blue Eyes gave them as a wedding present a little glass pipe, which, whenever he played it, brought the spring into the hearts of all who heard it. And Blue Eyes promised that whenever Blue Boy whistled on the pipe, he and Rainbow would immediately answer his call and come to him.

When the wedding was over, Blue Eyes gave Rainbow his scarf, and they mounted on two winged steeds and galloped off through the lanes. Now if you ever meet in a wood or by a river a man with blue eyes, on a winged horse, with a crown of dew, and a tunic of snowdrops and cowslips, and by his side, on a white pony, a beautiful woman wearing the rainbow for a scarf, and holding a branch of blossom in her hand, you will know it is Blue Eyes and Rainbow.

And if ever you hear on a spring morning, in a city or a village, three little notes played on a pipe which make your heart dance for joy, you will know that Blue Boy is calling for his father and his mother; for he does this very often.

Once upon a time there lived in China a wise Emperor, whose daughter was remarkable for her perfect beauty. Her feet were the smallest in the world; her eyes were long and slanting, and as bright as brown onyxes, and when you heard her laugh it was like listening to a tinkling stream, or to the chimes of a silver bell. Moreover, the Emperor's daughter was as wise as she was beautiful, and she chanted the verse of the great poets better than any one in the land. The Emperor was old in years; his son was married and had begotten a son; he was, therefore, quite happy about the succession to the throne, but he wished before he died to see his daughter wedded to some one who should be worthy of her.

Many suitors presented themselves at the palace, as soon as it became known that the Emperor desired a son-in-law, but when they reached the palace, they were met by the Lord Chamberlain, who told them the Emperor had decided that only the man who found and brought back the Blue Rose should marry his daughter. The suitors were much puzzled by this order. What was the Blue Rose, and where was it to be found? In all a hundred and fifty suitors had presented themselves, and out of these, fifty at once put away from them all thought of winning the hand of the Emperor's daughter, since they considered the condition imposed to be absurd.

The other hundred set about trying to find the Blue Rose. One of them—his name was Ti-Fun-Ti, he was a merchant and immensely rich—went at once to the largest shop in the town and said to the shopkeeper: "I want a blue rose, the best you have."

The shopkeeper, with many apologies, explained that he did not stock blue roses. He had red roses in profusion, white, pink, and yellow roses, but no blue rose. There had hitherto been no demand for the article.

"Well," said Ti-Fun-Ti, "you must get one for me. I do not mind how much money it costs, but I must have a blue rose."

The shopkeeper said he would do his best, but he feared it would be an expensive article and difficult to procure.

Another of the suitors, whose name I have forgotten, was a warrior and extremely brave; he mounted his horse, and taking with him a hundred archers and a thousand horsemen he marched into the territory of the King of Five Rivers, whom he knew to be the richest king in the world and the possessor of the rarest treasures, and demanded of him the Blue Rose, threatening him with a terrible doom should he be reluctant to give it up.

The King of the Five Rivers, who disliked soldiers, and had a horror of noise, violence, and every kind of fuss (his bodyguard was armed solely with fans and sunshades), rose from the cushions on which he was lying when the demand was made, and, tinkling a small bell, said to the servant who straightway appeared, "Fetch me the Blue Rose."

The servant retired and returned presently bearing on a silken cushion a large sapphire which was carved so as to imitate a full-blown rose with all its petals.

"This," said the King of the Five Rivers, "is the Blue Rose. You are welcome to it."

The warrior took it, and after making brief, soldier-like thanks, he went straight back to the Emperor's palace, saying that he had lost no time in finding the Blue Rose. He was ushered into the presence of the Emperor, who as soon as he heard the warrior's story and saw the Blue Rose which had been brought, sent for his daughter and said to her: "This intrepid warrior has brought you what he claims to be the Blue Rose. Has he accomplished the quest?"

The Princess took the precious object in her hands, and after examining it for a moment, said: "This is not a rose at all. It is a sapphire; I have no need of precious stones." And she returned the stone to the warrior, with many elegantly-expressed thanks. And the warrior went away in discomfiture.

When Ti-Fun-Ti, the merchant, heard of the warrior's failure, he was all the more anxious to win the prize. He sought the shopkeeper and said to him: "Have you got me the Blue Rose? I trust you have; because if not, I shall most assuredly be the means of your death. My brother-in-law is chief magistrate, and I am allied by marriage to all the chief officials in the kingdom."

The shopkeeper turned pale and said: "Sir, give me three days, and I will procure you the Blue Rose without fail." The merchant granted him the three days and went away. Now the shopkeeper was at his wit's end as to what to do, for he knew well there was no such thing as a blue rose. For two days he did nothing but moan and wring his hands, and on the third day he went to his wife and said: "Wife, we are ruined!"

But his wife, who was a sensible woman, said: "Nonsense! If there is no such thing as a blue rose we must make one. Go to the apothecary and ask him for a strong dye which will change a white rose into a blue one."

So the shopkeeper went to the apothecary and asked him for a dye, and the chemist gave him a bottle of red liquid, telling him to pick a white rose and to dip its stalk into the liquid and the rose would turn blue. The shopkeeper did as he was told; the rose turned into a beautiful blue and the shopkeeper took it to the merchant, who at once went with it to the palace, saying that he had found the Blue Rose.

He was ushered into the presence of the Emperor, who as soon as he saw the blue rose sent for his daughter and said to her: "This wealthy merchant has brought you what he claims to be the Blue Rose. Has he accomplished the quest?"

The Princess took the flower in her hands, and after examining it for a moment said: "This is a white rose; its stalk has been dipped in a poisonous dye and it has turned blue. Were a butterfly to settle upon it, it would die of the potent fume. Take it back. I have no need of a dyed rose." And she returned it to the merchant with many elegantly-expressed thanks.

The other ninety-eight suitors all sought in various ways for the Blue Rose. Some of them travelled all over the world seeking it; some of them sought the aid of wizards and astrologers, and one did not hesitate to invoke the help of the dwarfs that live underground. But all of them, whether they travelled in far countries, or took counsel with wizards and demons, or sat pondering in lonely places, failed to find the Blue Rose.

At last they all abandoned the quest except the Lord Chief Justice, who was the most skilful lawyer and statesman in the country. After thinking over the matter for several months, he sent for the most skilful artist in the country and said to him: "Make me a china cup. Let it be milk-white in colour and perfect in shape, and paint on it a rose, a blue rose."

The artist made obeisance and withdrew, and worked for two months at the Lord Chief Justice's cup. In two months' time it was finished, and the world has never seen such a beautiful cup, so perfect in symmetry, so delicate in texture, and the rose on it, the blue rose, was a living flower, picked in fairyland and floating on the rare milky surface of the porcelain. When the Lord Chief Justice saw it he gasped with surprise and pleasure, for he was a great lover of porcelain, and never in his life had he seen such a piece. He said to himself: "Without doubt the Blue Rose is here on this cup, and nowhere else."

So, after handsomely rewarding the artist, he went to the Emperor's palace and said that he had brought the Blue Rose. He was ushered into the Emperor's presence, who as he saw the cup sent for his daughter and said to her: "This eminent lawyer has brought you what he claims to be the Blue Rose. Has he accomplished the quest?"

The Princess took the bowl in her hands, and after examining it for a moment, said: "This bowl is the most beautiful piece of china I have ever seen. If you are kind enough to let me keep it I will put it aside until I receive the blue rose. For so beautiful is it that no other flower is worthy to be put in it except the Blue Rose."

The Lord Chief Justice thanked the Princess for accepting the bowl with many elegantly-turned phrases, and he went away in discomfiture.

After this there was no one in the whole country who ventured on the quest of the Blue Rose. It happened that not long after the Lord Chief Justice's attempt, a strolling minstrel visited the kingdom of the Emperor. One evening he was playing his one-stringed instrument outside a dark wall. It was a summer's evening, and the sun had sunk in a glory of dusty gold, and in the violet twilight one or two stars were twinkling like spear-heads. There was an incessant noise made by the croaking of frogs and the chatter of grasshoppers. The minstrel was singing a short song over and over again to a monotonous tune. The sense of it was something like this:—

"I watched beside the willow trees
The river, as the evening fell;
The twilight came and brought no breeze,
No dew, no water for the well,

"When from the tangled banks of grass,
A bird across the water flew,
And in the river's hard grey glass
I saw a flash of azure blue."

As he sang he heard a rustle on the wall, and looking up he saw a slight figure, white against the twilight, beckoning to him. He walked along under the wall until he came to a gate, and there some one was waiting for him, and he was gently led into the shadow of a dark cedar tree. In the twilight he saw two bright eyes looking at him, and he understood their message. In the twilight a thousand meaningless nothings were whispered in the light of the stars, and the hours fled swiftly. When the East began to grow light, the Princess (for it was she) said it was time to go.

"But," said the minstrel, "to-morrow I shall come to the palace and ask for your hand."

"Alas!" said the Princess, "I would that were possible, but my father has made a foolish condition that only he may wed me who finds the Blue Rose."

"That is simple," said the minstrel, "I will find it!" And they said good-night to each other.

The next morning the minstrel went to the palace, and on his way he picked a common white rose from a wayside garden. He was ushered into the Emperor's presence, who sent for his daughter and said to her: "This penniless minstrel has brought you what he claims to be the Blue Rose. Has he accomplished the quest?"

The Princess took the rose in her hands and said: "Yes, this is without doubt the Blue Rose."

But the Lord Chief Justice and all who were present respectfully pointed out that the rose was a common white rose and not a blue one, and the objection was with many forms and phrases conveyed to the Princess.

"I think the rose is blue," said the Princess. "It is, in fact, the Blue Rose. Perhaps you are all colour blind."

The Emperor, with whom the decision rested, decided that if the Princess thought the rose was blue, it was blue, for it was well known that her perception was more acute than that of any one else in the kingdom.

So the minstrel married the Princess, and they settled on the sea-coast in a little green house with a garden full of white roses, and they lived happily for ever afterwards. And the Emperor, knowing that his daughter had made a good match, died in peace.

THE STORY OF VOX ANGELICA AND LIEBLICH GEDACHT

Once upon a time there was a poor tanner called Hans who lived with his wife Martha in a town in which there were two hundred churches, a hundred chapels, and a huge cathedral.

Hans lived in a wooden house opposite the gates of the cathedral. They had only one son and he was so delicate that they did not know what trade he could learn when he grew bigger. In the meantime they taught him how to read and write. The boy was christened Johan; for he was born on St. John's Day. When Johan was quite a tiny little boy he liked listening to the sound of the organ in the big cathedral, and in the evenings he would sit for hours in the darkness, listening to the organist at his practice.

The organist was an old man called Doctor Sebastian, and he wore a powdered wig and large tortoise-shell spectacles. When he played the organ, which was an immense instrument and had five keyboards, the windows trembled in all the houses which nestled round the cathedral.

Doctor Sebastian soon noticed the little Johan and allowed him to come up into the organ-loft while he was playing, and Johan used to sit as still as a mouse, and watch him pull out the stops, and play with his feet as skilfully as he did with his hands. Doctor Sebastian had a pupil called Frantz, a lad with curly brown hair and large brown eyes. Frantz used to practise on the organ every day; but Doctor Sebastian was severe with him, and Frantz was not allowed to play the organ at High Mass on Sundays. One day Johan asked Doctor Sebastian whether this was because Frantz played badly, and Doctor Sebastian said:

"Frantz has much to learn and he must be trained, but one day, when he has learnt all that I can teach him, he will be able to teach me what I shall not be able to learn."

Johan did not understand what this meant, but he guessed that Doctor Sebastian thought well of Frantz, in spite of his being so severe with him. Johan thought that Frantz was the most wonderful player in the world, and whereas Doctor Sebastian only made the organ speak in deep single tones, and only used the open stops and the booming pedal bass-notes, Frantz—when Doctor Sebastian was not there to listen—used to make the organ sigh and speak like a castle full of spirits, and Johan thought this was wonderful.

One day, it was in winter just before Christmas, and Johan was eight years old, Doctor Sebastian was laid up in bed with a bad cold, and he sent for Frantz and said to him:

"I shall never rise from my bed again. I am going thither where I shall hear the music which we only guess at here on earth. You must play the organ on Christmas Day. I have taught you all I know. I have been severe and gruff with you; but being a musician, you know that if I had not thought you worthy of it, I should not have taken any trouble with you at all. I have been spared until you were ready to take my place, and now I can go in peace, for I know that I leave behind me a worthy successor. I have scolded you and pulled your ears, rapped your fingers and blamed your playing, but you have got that which I should never learn if I lived for two hundred years. You have the divine gift, and as a musician I am not worthy to unlatch the shoes of what you will be; for you will play on earth the music that I am now going to hear in Heaven!"

After that Doctor Sebastian squeezed Frantz's hand and said no more. The next day he died.

Frantz was very sad, and he spent the whole day that the Doctor died in the cathedral composing a requiem in memory of his dead master. Little Johan, in a corner of the aisle, listened to the music: he had never heard anything so beautiful; some new power seemed to have come to Frantz, and when he touched the keys the pipes spoke in a way they had never spoken before.

Frantz went on playing until late into the night, and Johan had been carried so far away into dreamland by the music that he did not notice when Frantz stopped, but all at once he became aware that he was alone in the cathedral and that the organ-loft was dark and no sound came from it.

Johan ran up the winding stair into the organ-loft, but Frantz had gone, and Johan knew that he was locked in the cathedral for the night. He made up his mind to sleep there where he was, and he was just taking one of Frantz's missals to use as a pillow when he became aware that he was no longer alone. Sitting on the bench in front of the keys was a strange figure. It was an old man with a grey beard, twinkling eyes, and a deep voice like the buzzing of a hornet. He wore a brown coat and grey stockings, and a black three-cornered hat.

"Who are you?" asked Johan.

"My name is Quint," said the little old man, "and I live in one of the big wooden pipes of the organ."

"Do you always live there?" asked Johan.

"No, not always," said Quint. "We don't live here as a rule, but some of them oblige us to come here and sing—"

"I don't understand," said Johan.

"Well, I will explain it to you," answered Quint. "It's like this: Every one of the stops of the organ has some one who belongs to it and to whom it belongs—but these people do not live in the stops; they live in their own country, which is called Musicland, and they only come to the organs when they are obliged to."

"But who obliges them?" asked Johan.

Quint thought for a moment, and then he said: "Those who have the gift."

"But what is the gift?" asked Johan.

"That I can't tell you," said Quint. "All I know is that some have it and others haven't."

"Did Doctor Sebastian have the gift?" asked Johan.

"No," said Quint, "he was a learned man and a very good man; but he hadn't got the gift. But young Frantz: he's got it. That's why I am here to-day."

"Are the people of the other stops here too?" asked Johan, who was deeply interested in what Quint told him.

"They've all gone home," said Quint. "You see, as long as the player plays, we can stay here and not come out except just when we're wanted; but if we don't get back into the pipes before the player has finished, we can't go home. Now just before Frantz finished I crept out of my pipe because I wasn't wanted, and I wished to look at the cathedral, and then suddenly he stopped playing, before I could get back into my pipe again, and if we are not in our pipes when the organist stops playing we can't get home."

"What will you do then?" asked Johan.

"I shall have to wait till he plays again to-morrow. I can get into a pipe of course, but I can't go home."

"To Musicland?" asked Johan.

"Yes," said Quint, "and it's annoying, because I shall miss the end of the wedding festivities."

"Whose wedding?" asked Johan.

"Vox Angelica's, of course," said Quint. "She was married yesterday."

"Vox Angelica is that lovely soft stop in the swell," said Johan. "I suppose she's going to marry 'Lieblich Gedacht'?"

"Of course she is," said Quint, "but it's a long business. If you like I will tell you all about it."

"Oh, please do!" said Johan.

"Well," began Quint, "Vox Angelica is the most beautiful person you have ever seen. Her eyes are just like blue waters, grave and still, and her hair is long and as bright as the gold on a harp. And as for her voice, well, you can hear that whenever Frantz plays the organ. She is as kind and gentle as she is beautiful, and everybody in our country loves her. She lives in that part of Musicland where the hills and white mountains are. In the winter it is covered with snow which gleams in the sunshine, whiter and brighter than any snow you have ever seen, but when the spring comes the snow disappears and the slopes of the mountains are covered with millions and millions of flowers which are soft and white and glisten like stars.

"Lieblich Gedacht was the son of a forester, and he lives in the Woods of Melody, right in the heart of our country where the old oak forests grow, which are carpeted with bluebells in the spring so that the enormous stems look as if they rose out of a blue sea, and in the spring and in the summer the woods are full of birds; but no bird there has so sweet a note as Lieblich Gedacht when he sings in the wood. The birds stop singing to listen to him. He sings all the year round: when the woods are green, and in the autumn too, when they are gold and crimson like the tattered banners of our King, and in the winter, when the oak trees spread their bare arms across the clear cold sky.

"One day Lieblich Gedacht put on a green jerkin, a green cap, and taking with him a sword and a pipe he set out on his travels. He wandered through Musicland until he came to a castle which was on the top of a mountain. This castle had a tower with one window in it, and from the window came the sound of a whisper which sounded so soft and wonderful that Lieblich Gedacht thought it must be the voice of a flower speaking to itself: the jessamine perhaps, or the briar rose. Then he looked up and he saw leaning out of the window a maid with gold hair which fell from the window far down the tower, and she was as frail and as lovely as a gentian on the mountains.

"Then Lieblich Gedacht sang a song. He sang of all the beautiful things he had ever dreamed of; he sang of the sun and the moon and the stars, of the spring, the grass, the great woods and their secret; he sang the song the leaves sing when they wake in the dawn, and the song the boughs sing in the evening when they lull the birds and the flowers to sleep. He sang of the love he felt for all the beautiful things in the world, and about how glad he was to be alive in a beautiful country like Musicland.

"Vox Angelica heard him, and answered his song, and they sang a duet together, and Lieblich Gedacht's part said, 'I love you,' and Vox Angelica's part said, 'I love you too.'

"Then Lieblich Gedacht asked Vox Angelica to marry him, and she said she would, and they settled they would start at once for the City of Pleasant Sounds and be married. They started at once. Lieblich Gedacht rode on a grey horse, and Vox Angelica rode on the saddle in front of him. Now their way lay through a perilous wood called the Forest of Discord, which was infested by imps called Chromatics, and by hundreds of gnomes who made a hideous noise, and in the middle of this wood lived Bourdon, who is a wizard.

"When they reached the wood it was already dark, and from every bush and tree came sharp sounds, ugly cries, moans, groans, squeaks, wheezes, and in the distance they could hear a deep buzzing boom.

"Vox Angelica and Lieblich Gedacht were rather frightened, since it was dark and neither of them knew the way, for neither of them had ever been near the Forest of Discord before, and they knew none of the people who belonged to it. So they made up their minds not to go any farther but to sleep under the shade of an oak-tree. It was summer, so it was warm. They made themselves a bed of leaves and lay down; but the Chromatics made such a noise that they could not go to sleep. At last they put moss into their ears so that they could not hear the ugly sounds, and they both fell asleep.

"In the middle of the night Lieblich Gedacht had a bad dream. He dreamed that the trees had come to life and had stretched out their arms and taken Vox Angelica away from him, and that when he tried to keep her they bound him down to the ground.

"When Lieblich Gedacht awoke, it was daylight and the sun was shining through the dark trees. But what was his grief and despair when he saw that Vox Angelica was no longer there! She had gone, disappeared, and left no trace. He looked for her everywhere; he called out her name in a thousand ways till the ugly wood re-echoed with the sweetness of his song, but no Vox Angelica answered. She was nowhere to be found. Lieblich Gedacht was in despair. He did not know what to do nor where to look. 'But,' he thought to himself, 'one thing is certain: it is no use wasting time in this forest, I must go and find some one who will be likely to help me.'

"So he rode out of the Forest of Discord as quickly as he could, and crossed the plains which lie beyond it, and he rode on until he reached the Wood of Dreams, which is on the other side of the plains.

"In this wood there lives a hermit called Sackbut, who is well known for his goodness and his wisdom, and Lieblich Gedacht made up his mind to go and ask him for his help and advice. Sackbut lives in a cave underground. He is very old, and has a long white beard six times as long as mine. Lieblich Gedacht, after searching for some time in the wood, found a clear space in the thickets, and in the middle of it a circle of built bricks which looked like the top of a well. But when he looked down into what he thought was the well he saw there were steps in it which went down underground. He went boldly down the steps and into the dark, and when he had counted thirty-two of them they stopped and he came to the door. He knocked at this door, and he heard a hoarse voice saying: 'Who is there?'

"'It is I, Lieblich Gedacht,' he answered. 'I have come for advice.'

"The door was opened at once, and Lieblich Gedacht found himself in a cell lit by a lantern, and in front of him, sitting at a table and reading a large book, which had nothing but notes in it, was Sackbut the Hermit.

"'Well, what do you want?' asked the hermit in a gruff voice. 'Be quick and tell me, because I am busy and I have got no time to waste. I am learning a fugue by one of those new-fangled German musicians, and I must know it by next Sunday, for there's a man in one of their cities who has the gift, and I shall have to go.'

"'I have plighted my troth to Vox Angelica,' said Lieblich Gedacht. 'We were travelling together to the City of Pleasant Sounds to be married, and we stopped on the way in the Forest of Discord.'

"'That was a silly thing to do,' said Sackbut.

"'We slept the night there, and when I woke up in the morning Vox Angelica had disappeared.'

"'Did you hear anything in the night?' asked Sackbut.

"'No,' said Lieblich Gedacht, 'but I had a bad nightmare. I dreamed the trees were taking her away and strangling me.'

"'I see,' said Sackbut, 'it's Bourdon the wizard; he's at his old tricks again. Vox Angelica has been carried away by Bourdon, and he has probably hidden her somewhere. He would not dare keep her in his castle, because the Chromatics are such gossips that the whole kingdom would know it at once. She is a prisoner somewhere; of that you can be sure. But where I cannot tell you. All I can advise you is to go and ask Echo: she hears everything.'

"'And where does Echo live?' asked Lieblich Gedacht.

"'Echo,' said Sackbut, 'lives in the Castle of the Winds, which is not very far away. You must go right through the Wood of Dreams, and across the plains, and then you will come to a valley; you must descend into this valley, which is steep, and climb up the other side of it; and there on a high rock you will see the Castle of the Winds. Good-bye.'

"And the Hermit bent over his music-book once more and hummed to himself in his deep bass voice. But just as Lieblich Gedacht was going away, Sackbut called him back and gave him a walnut, and said: 'Whenever you are in danger and want my help, crack this. Now go.'

"Lieblich Gedacht thanked Sackbut, and did as he had been told. He rode through the Wood of Dreams, which is a quiet wood, shady and dim. There are very few birds in it; but the nightingale sings there all day and the nightjar sings there all night. And on his way he passed a cottage where Waldhorn the hunter lives, and farther on he passed a castle which belongs to Waldflöte the Lord of the Forest. But neither of them were at home; for Waldhorn was out hunting, and Waldflöte was on a visit to his cousin Cor de Nuit, who lives in the Orchards of Twilight.

"Lieblich Gedacht soon reached the valley, which is deep and made of great rocks and quarries. It is so steep that he had to lead his horse down the whole way. But the other side was easier to climb because it was grassy, and he was able to ride up it. When he reached the top, he saw a castle with transparent walls which reflected the sunlight and which had hundreds of windows, all of them wide open so as to let in the winds from all the corners of the world. When he reached the door he sang a soft note, and he immediately heard it repeated hundreds and hundreds of times so that the whole world seemed to be full of calling sounds. The door opened of itself, and Lieblich walked into a hall, at the end of which was a winding staircase. He walked up this staircase and he went on and on until he thought it would never end. At last he came to the top, and there, in a little room which had eight sides, sitting on a crystal throne, was Echo.

"She was dressed in moonbeams and dewdrops and the fleece of a cloud, and she had wings made of gossamer like those of a dragon-fly, and on her head there trembled a star.

"'I have come,' said Lieblich Gedacht, 'to ask you to help me.' And he told his story.

"'Two nights ago,' said Echo when he had finished, 'I heard Bourdon start from his castle in his large rumbling coach. His horses were galloping. He left his castle and drove for some time through the Forest of Discord, and then he stopped. At that moment I heard a sigh which I am sure was Vox Angelica speaking. But the sigh was soon stifled, and Bourdon drove off again in his coach. He drove right through the Forest of Dreams, over the plains, till he came to the sea, and there he got out and disappeared under the sea. After that I do not know what happened, because the winds cannot bring me any news of what happens underneath the sea; but he probably crossed the sea and went to Muteland, which is beyond it. But I advise you to go and ask Unda Maris, who lives under the sea. She will tell you.'

"'But how shall I find Unda Maris?' asked Lieblich Gedacht.

"'All you have got to do is to go to the seashore,' said Echo; 'you must take this ring, and when you get there'—and here she gave Lieblich Gedacht a silver ring with a strange blue stone in it—'you must throw it into the sea and sing—

"Ring, ring, go home,
To the fishes and the foam;
Say the word and open the sea,
Come and show the way to me."

But remember this: if any one asks you to do them a service, however small, which might delay your journey, you must refuse, or evil will come of it. And you had better take this with you, and whenever you are in danger and want my help, open it.' And she gave Lieblich Gedacht a little green egg.

"Lieblich Gedacht thanked Echo and said good-bye, and then he rode as quickly as he could to the seashore. There he threw the ring into the sea and said—

'Ring, ring, go home,
To the fishes and the foam;
Say the word and open the sea,
Come and show the way to me.'

No sooner had he said this than the sea opened wide, and he saw before him a stone staircase with a rope made of pearls for him to walk down by; and a silver fish with webbed feet and hands went in front of him and showed him the way.

"The fish led him a long walk right to the bottom of the sea, and when he got there, he found a place built of rocks and seaweeds. Inside it was green and dim like a summer night, and sounds echoed through its green corridors. The fish led Lieblich Gedacht through many halls to the central grotto, which was built of sapphires, where Unda Maris lived. She was lying on a bed of purple seaweed when he entered the grotto, and she was touching the strings of a golden harp. She was almost hidden by a veil, and her face shone behind it, pale like the moon behind a cloud. She asked Lieblich Gedacht what he wanted, and he told his story.

"'It is true,' she said when he had finished. 'Bourdon has carried away Vox Angelica out of Musicland. He passed through the sea three days ago—passed through and took her to Muteland beyond the sea, to the Castle of Silence that stands in the middle of the Lake of Sighs. You must go there if you wish to find her. You must cross the sea to get there in a boat, and you must be sure on no account to stop anywhere on the way, or else evil will come of it. Take this with you, and whenever you are in danger, and want my help, open it.' So saying, she gave Lieblich Gedacht a pearly shell.

"So Lieblich Gedacht thanked Unda Maris and said good-bye, and walked back by the staircase to the seashore again. When he got there the first thing he did was to go to a fisherman's hut and ask him to lend him a boat to cross the sea in. While he was talking to the fisherman he saw three figures coming towards him. One was dressed in bright armour, and wore a gold cloak on his left shoulder, and a crimson cap with a crimson feather in it, and a sword. This was Prince Hautboy, and with him was his page, Piccolo, a mischievous little boy with beady brown eyes, clothed entirely in silver; and the second, who wore a scarlet tunic and who carried a broadsword and a bugle, was Cornet the soldier; and the third was a tall figure with a handsome, melancholy face, dressed in black velvet and wearing a large black cap from which a proud white plume waved. This was Viol d'Amore, the brave nobleman who was a swordsman and who made beautiful verses and sang them.

"Lieblich Gedacht walked up to them, and taking off his green cap made obeisance to them.

"Hautboy and Viol d'Amore asked him who he was.

"'I am Lieblich Gedacht,' he said, 'the son of the forester. I live in the Woods of Melody, and I am betrothed to Vox Angelica. But Bourdon has taken her away and locked her up in the Castle of Silence on the Lake of Sighs, and I am going to rescue her.'

"'Then you can come with us,' said Hautboy, 'for we are bound upon a like errand. I am betrothed to Clarabella, and Bourdon has taken her away; and Viol d'Amore is looking for Dolce his betrothed, and Cornet for Muzette, who is pledged to him, and Bourdon has taken them too.'

"So Viol d'Amore, Hautboy, Cornet, and Lieblich Gedacht, and Piccolo the page, got into the boat, hoisted the sail and set out to sea. They had a fair breeze, and for three days their voyage continued smoothly without any adventures; but on the fourth day they met a huge brass ship with a serpent at the prow which challenged them.

"'This is Bourdon's doing,' said Hautboy; 'he has had wind of our adventure and sent his allies against us.'

"In the brass ship there were two very fearsome warriors—Tromba, who was a giant mailed in brazen armour, like the vessel, and Bassoon, who was as large as a barrel and who had a voice like thunder; and with them were fifty tin soldiers. As soon as the vessel approached, Tromba cried out in a ringing voice—

"'Surrender, you are my prisoners!'

"'In whose name?' cried out Hautboy.

"'In the name of Bourdon, our King,' answered Tromba.

"'We recognise no king save King Diapason, our lawful sovereign,' said Hautboy unabashed.

"'Then if you won't surrender we shall make you,' said Tromba; and he told his soldiers to ram the little boat.

"Hautboy thought that all was lost; and Lieblich Gedacht said, 'If only Unda Maris were here she could help us.' Then he remembered the shell which she had given to him, and he opened it. There was nothing inside it except a tiny seed-pearl, and as he opened the shell the vessel gave a lurch and the seed-pearl fell into the sea. Lieblich Gedacht cried out in despair, but as he did so, a wave rose between them and the brazen vessel, and from out this wave came a gigantic sea-serpent, which at once attacked the brazen vessel. Tromba and Bassoon were frightened out of their wits, and setting all sail they fled as fast as they could, and their ship was soon out of sight. Then the sea-serpent disappeared, and the sea at once became quite calm again. They journeyed on for two more days, and the weather grew warmer and finer every hour, and the sky turned to a softer azure, and the sea to a deeper blue; they were borne along by the lightest of breezes, and sometimes their sail flapped idly in the still air.

"On the third day, they descried a speck of land on the horizon, and towards the evening they could see that it was an island with misty hills and lights on it. All round it on the sea, which the sunset had turned fiery, little white sails seemed to be scudding towards it, and when the sun set and the stars came out there came to them from the island a faint thread of wonderful sound.

"Hautboy and Cornet said they thought it would be a good thing to land at this island for the night, and Lieblich Gedacht was so curious to hear more of the lovely music that he forgot all about the warning Unda Maris had given him not to stop anywhere on the way, and he consented.

"So they ran their boat into a sandy cove, hauled her up on to the beach, and landed. The island was overgrown with tall ferns; and shapes of trees, such as none of them had ever seen before, nodded to them from the hills. There appeared to be no birds, beasts, or any living creature on the island, but the thread of sound they had heard in the distance, was fuller now and more silvery, and they walked up along a grassy path towards the place where it seemed to come from. After they had climbed up the ground in front of them for some time, they reached a spot where the ground ceased to rise. Lieblich Gedacht turned round to have one last look at the sea before walking down into the valley which was before them. The stars twinkled in the sky and the sea mirrored them like quiet glass, and strange to say, all the little white sails which they had seen at sunset scudding round the island had disappeared.

"They went down into the valley, and the ferns became more dusky and taller, the path darker and darker, and the sound of music sweeter and more insistent; they crossed the valley, and the pathway led them uphill once more to a clear space, and before them rose pinnacles and domes all grey and shimmering like a mist which hides the sun, and in this frail dwelling-place a hundred little lights glistened like glowworms, and the whole place trembled with the magical silvery sound which they had followed.

"They walked on, and they came to a grey portal with colours in it like those of a fading rainbow, and a voice bade them enter. They did so, and found themselves beneath a cloudy dome, so high that they could not see the top of it, and although there were myriads of small lights twinkling everywhere, the air remained dim and mysterious: but the sound was louder and clearer. They could not but follow it, and it led them beyond the dome up a flight of steps to a terrace which was open to the sky. The terrace was long and broad, and as unreal and unsubstantial as though it were built of moonshine. They walked on, straight in front of them, until they came to a transparent wall. They looked over this, and beneath them was a steep slope covered with grasses and ferns, trees and plants; down this slope, which was interrupted at intervals by the outline of smaller terraces and ledges, in which were sheets of light, like pools of water, they seemed to hear a hundred waterfalls rushing whispering down the slope; and far away in the darkness they saw the ghosts of white fountains rising and sobbing. On their left, the terrace overlooked the sea, and went sheer down to the beach; and on their right, tall shadows hid from their view the fern-forests of the island. In the air there was scent of flowers, and the whole terrace was overgrown with some sweet jessamine-like flower which they could not see, for both the terrace and the sloping garden beneath them were shrouded in a mist in which millions and millions of fireflies swarmed and glistened. And all this time the sound grew softer, clearer, and stronger. Just as they were wondering where it could be coming from, there came to them from out and through the filmy walls of the dwelling, a beautiful lady. Her face was like a pale flower, and her hair, which fell to her feet, was dark as the night, and she was dressed in clinging folds of dewy silver, and she stretched out her white arms to them and said in a voice which seemed like that of the summer darkness—

"'Welcome!' Then she led them into the house, up into a high room, built in the clouds and from which they could see the circle of the island and the sea beyond.

"They at once fell into a deep sleep, and in their dreams winged shapes fanned them and soft voices whispered to them. The next morning when they awoke, although the sun was shining the mists did not rise from the island; everything remained filmy, grey, and dim, shimmering like a bell of foam; lights twinkled and fountains and waterfalls plashed, and the island echoed with hidden voices and the same magical sound.

"'I suppose,' said Lieblich Gedacht, 'we ought to go on with our journey?'

"'Yes,' said Hautboy, 'but where are we going to?'

"'Yes, where are we going to?' repeated Cornet.

"And Lieblich Gedacht thought and thought, and puzzled and puzzled; but neither he nor any of them could remember where they were going. Presently Hautboy said—

"'Why should we go anywhere? What place could be better than this island?'

"'This is better than fighting,' said Cornet.

"'And then making verses and singing them,' said Viol d'Amore.

"'And then piping all day,' said Piccolo.

"'Nobody asked your opinion,' said Hautboy.

"And so they wandered about in this magical island, listening to the delicious sound and smelling flowers which they could not see; they were steeped in the mist of the place, and they could not remember what it was they had set out to do. They were captives to the dream and the spell of the place, and however much they tried they could not drive the mist from their minds and remember what they had set out to do. At sunset the beautiful lady appeared again and gave them fruits to eat and water in a crystal cup, and she sang to them a song, and never had they heard anything so lovely. When she had done singing, Lieblich Gedacht asked her who she was and what the island was called.

"She said: 'I am the daughter of the moon, and this island is called the Island of Moon Dew. I am very lonely, but you shall keep me company now.'

"'But,' said Lieblich Gedacht, 'we must not stay here long. We are bound on a quest, only we can't remember just now exactly what it is.'

"'We will talk of that later,' said the lady, 'in the meantime I will sing you a song.' And she sang them to sleep with her wonderful voice.

"A whole year passed, and every day was spent in the same way, in dream and song and sleep. Cornet, Hautboy, and Viol d'Amore had quite stopped worrying about their journey, and about what they should do in the future. But Lieblich Gedacht was sad because he knew there was something he ought to do, but he could not remember what it was. One day when he was wandering by himself in the gardens of the island, he sat down to rest on the grass beside some misty bushes. He was trying hard to remember, and he happened to take out of his pocket the little egg which Echo had given him. He had quite forgotten what it was, and he played with it, throwing it up and catching it; and then growing tired of this game, he put the egg on the grass next to the misty bushes so that it touched one of them. Directly he did this a myrtle bush, which had not been there before, appeared out of the mist quite distinct, and it at once began to speak.

"'Who are you,' it said, 'who have made me visible and given me the power to speak?'

"'I am Lieblich Gedacht,' he answered. 'I have been here a year, and what I am doing I don't know, because I can't remember things.'

"'You are protected by some powerful spell,' said the myrtle, 'or else you would have suffered my fate already. Don't you know where you are?'

"'No,' said Lieblich Gedacht, 'we came here in a boat one evening after sunset; we have seen the Lady of the Island, but we do not know her name.'

"'Then I will tell you,' said the myrtle. 'You are in the island of Zauberflöte the enchantress. All who come here lose their memory and forget their homes, their native country, and the faces that they love. And when they have been here a year, Zauberflöte puts them to the test. She bids them listen to the Moon Song, and if they can listen to it without falling asleep, they are free, but if they fall asleep, then they are hers for ever, and she changes them into ghostly shapes: plants, fountains, streams, waterfalls, flowers, trees, ferns, or whatever she wishes.'

"'And who are you?' asked Lieblich Gedacht.

"'I,' said the myrtle, 'am the youngest son of the Sleeping Beauty in the wood. I was on my way to Musicland to seek adventure. I stopped at this island, although my fairy godmother had warned me not to, and after I had been here a year Zauberflöte sang me the Moon Song and I fell asleep, and she changed me into a myrtle bush. There are many, many people on this island who have suffered the same fate. From my country there are the Marquis of Carrabas, who stayed here for a night to feed his cat: he is changed into a fuchsia and the cat into a tiger-lily; and Cinderella is here too: she was changed into a glass slipper; and there are many knights and maidens from all the corners of the world, sleeping here in the shape of ghostly ferns and trees and flowers.'

"'What must I do?' he asked, 'to resist the Moon Song?'

"'It is very difficult,' said the myrtle, 'no one has ever resisted it yet; but you must have some spell about you or else you could not have made me visible and given me speech. But look, what is that egg lying on the grass next to my stem?'

"'Oh, Echo gave me that,' said Lieblich Gedacht; 'I had forgotten, but I remember now; she told me to crush it if I was in danger!'

"'You must not crush it until the Moon Song has begun,' said the myrtle, 'and then the spell will be broken, and we shall all be free, for as soon as some one is found who can resist the Moon Song, the spell will cease to bind us; but if you don't break the egg in time, you will sleep here for ever. Now I must not talk any more or else we shall be discovered.'

"Lieblich Gedacht thanked the myrtle and went away. That night there was a full moon, and never had the island looked so beautiful. Zauberflöte came on to the terrace, and called Hautboy, Cornet, Viol d'Amore, Lieblich Gedacht and Piccolo, and said she would sing to them.

"She began to sing the Moon Song, and never had her voice been so silvery and never had they listened to such a song; all the island was trembling with joy, and the moon and the stars seemed to be leaning out of the sky to listen. And just as Lieblich Gedacht was yielding to the spell and sinking into a delicious ocean of dreams he cracked the egg to pieces between his fingers.

"At that moment the song stopped, and Lieblich Gedacht heard the echo of Vox Angelica's voice, which came from the egg, sighing: 'Lieblich Gedacht, my betrothed, have you forgotten me?'

"'Of course I haven't,' said Lieblich Gedacht. 'Come, Hautboy, Viol d'Amore, and Cornet, we are bound for Bourdon's castle.' At that moment Viol d'Amore, Hautboy, and Cornet remembered everything they had forgotten and whither they were bound.

"As Lieblich Gedacht said this, Zauberflöte disappeared at once into her mysterious palace. The mists lifted and vanished and the garden appeared in its true shape, just like an ordinary garden, with stone terraces overgrown with jessamine, and trees and bushes, and flowers and grass and weeds, just like anywhere else, and the shadows on one side of the terrace were cypress trees, and Zauberflöte's palace was an ordinary palace built of marble. From the garden came Prince Myrtle, the Marquis of Carrabas, Cinderella, and a hundred other knights and maidens who had been spellbound there for years; and they all thanked Lieblich Gedacht for setting them free. They started at once in their boats, which they found in the cove where they had left them. The Marquis of Carrabas, Prince Myrtle, and Cinderella set out for Musicland, and Lieblich Gedacht and his comrades started once more on their quest of rescue.

"They sailed for three more days and for three more nights, and they arrived at Muteland. Muteland is a flat country with no woods in it and very few trees, and those have no leaves on them. Some people say this is so that they may not rustle. But they couldn't rustle even if they had leaves, because there is no wind in Muteland. There are no birds in Muteland, and the only beasts there are dormice and salamanders. There are no streams and no rivers, and the people who live there only speak to each other by signs. In the middle of the country there is a large lake called the Lake of Sighs, because some people say that the sound of sighs is sometimes heard coming from it, and that these are the only sounds which have ever been heard in the country.

"As soon as Hautboy, Viol d'Amore, Cornet, Piccolo, and Lieblich Gedacht landed on the coast of Muteland, the first thing they did was to sing a song. This frightened the people there so much that they all ran into their holes; for the inhabitants of Muteland live underground. They walked for some hours over the barren plains until they came to an avenue of leafless willows. Lieblich Gedacht was walking on ahead, and as he passed one of these trees he stopped, for he thought he heard a human moan coming from one of the trees. He paused and listened, and again the sound was repeated. This time he heard it quite plainly. It was the piteous and musical moan of a human creature in pain. It trembled through the silence, and shook and quivered and touched Lieblich Gedacht's kind heart.

"He walked up to the tree which was nearest to him to see if he could find out where the noise came from. Then from above, coming from the heart of the tree, he heard the plaintive voice crying to him: 'Release me. Set me free. I am imprisoned in the trunk of this tree.'

"'Who are you?' asked Lieblich Gedacht.

"'I am Vox Humana,' said the voice, 'I was imprisoned in this tree by a wizard a hundred years ago, and nobody will set me free.'

"'But how can I set you free?' asked Lieblich Gedacht.

"'All you have got to do is to touch the tree and say—

"Willow-tree, willow-tree,
Hark to me, hark!
Set the poor captive free,
Open your bark.'"

"Lieblich Gedacht in his distress quite forgot what Echo had told him about not delaying his journey to render any one a service, and he touched the tree and said the words.

"As soon as he had done this, the tree opened and Vox Humana came out of it, with tears of gratitude in her soft brown eyes; but the spell which the wizard had put on the tree was of such a kind that he who set free a prisoner from it became a prisoner himself, and Vox Humana did not know this. So directly she was set free, Lieblich Gedacht found himself in her place, a prisoner in the dark trunk of the willow-tree, and although Vox Humana, who was very unselfish, at once touched the tree, and said the magic rhyme, because she preferred to be imprisoned herself rather than to cause some one else to be a captive, the spell did not work a second time. Indeed, like most spells, it could only be used once.

"Presently Hautboy, Viol d'Amore and Cornet came up, and they found Vox Humana crying bitterly. She told them what had happened, and they did not know what to do, for they could not even hear Lieblich Gedacht's voice; because it is only after years and years that a person who is imprisoned in a tree can be heard by any one else. And that is the reason why Vox Humana has such a plaintive voice. They were all very sad, and they settled to go on to the Lake of Sighs and accomplish their quest, and then perhaps they would find some way of setting Lieblich Gedacht free again. They soon reached the Lake of Sighs, and in the middle of it, on a rocky island, stood the Castle of Silence. They found a boat on the shore of the lake, and it carried them across by itself, without oars or sail. They found the gates of the castle (which was all black) wide open. They entered the castle. It was quite empty and deserted. They went into room after room. They searched every nook and corner, but they found nothing. When they came to the banqueting-hall they found a meal ready for them, with fruits and bread and wine, which were served by invisible hands; so they sat down and ate, for they were hungry.

"When they had had enough they began to search the castle once more, but they soon felt sleepy, so they lay down in one of the rooms where they found beds all ready for them, and fell fast asleep.

"No sooner were they asleep than Bourdon's three cousins, Bass, Violone, and Ophicleide, who were looking after the castle for him, and who had been hiding in a secret room in the walls, came out and bound them and cast them into an oubliette which was at the bottom of the castle, right under the lake. And there they found Vox Angelica, Dolce, Muzette, and Clarabella.

"To go back to Lieblich Gedacht: he was of course miserable, and he spent a whole month in the willow-tree, waiting for Hautboy and the others to come to set him free. But they never came. At last one day he remembered the walnut which Sackbut had given him. He had quite forgotten it up to that moment. He took it out of his pocket and cracked it, and in it he found a tiny silver key and a hazel nut. He put the hazel nut in his pocket, and he looked everywhere in the tree for a keyhole, and at last he found a tiny crack; he put the key in the crack and it fitted exactly. The door of the tree opened and he was free once more. He set out for the lake at once, and reached it in a few hours. Exactly the same things happened to him as to the others. The boat took him across the lake. He entered the empty castle and explored every nook and corner of it, but he found nothing. When he came into the banqueting-hall he saw the table spread by invisible hands; but he said to himself: 'I will not eat and drink till I have found Vox Angelica.' So he did not touch the food; but he went on searching. As he was looking out of one of the windows of the castle he distinctly heard Vox Angelica's sigh coming from the lake, and he at once understood that she was imprisoned in some dungeon underneath the lake. He waited until it was dark, and then he took the boat and rowed round the castle, and low down by the water he came to a barred window, and from this window came the sound of many sighs. Lieblich Gedacht now understood why the lake was called the Lake of Sighs, for the sighs came from prisoners imprisoned in Bourdon's dungeon.

"'Is that you, Vox Angelica?' he whispered.

"'Yes,' she whispered back, 'we are all here in the dungeon. But you must be careful, because Bourdon's three brothers are hiding in the castle.'

"'How can I rescue you?' asked Lieblich Gedacht.

"'I don't know,' said Vox Angelica. 'We are all of us bound in fetters.'

"'I will try and find a file,' said Lieblich Gedacht, 'to file the bars of the window and set you free.'

"So he went back to the castle to look for a file, but as he entered the gate Bourdon's three brothers fell upon him, and bound him, and cast him into the dungeon.

"'Alas!' said Vox Humana, 'we are all lost now.'

"'Not at all!' said Lieblich Gedacht, 'we will soon be free. Piccolo is so small he ought to be able to wriggle out of his chains, which are much too big for him.'

"Piccolo needed no further telling, and he soon managed to set himself free.

"'Now we are no better off than before,' said Vox Humana, who was always inclined to take a gloomy view of things. But Piccolo was then told to look in Lieblich Gedacht's pocket for a hazel nut, and when he found it to crack it. Piccolo found the nut, cracked it, and inside the nut tightly rolled up was a silk cap.

"'Now,' said Lieblich Gedacht, 'you must put the cap on my head.' As soon as Piccolo did this, Lieblich Gedacht's chains fell from him and he was free. For the cap was of that kind which makes a man invisible, unchainable, and as strong as ten. The next thing he did was to break the fetters of the eight other prisoners; then he pulled the bars from the window. They could not get out, but in front of the window were the waters of the lake, and they had no boat.

"'Perhaps,' said Lieblich Gedacht, 'the hazel nut will help us again because it is faëry,' and he took half the nutshell and threw it into the lake. It at once turned into a boat just big enough to hold Vox Humana, Vox Angelica, Clarabella, Dolce, Muzette, Hautboy, Cornet, Viol d'Amore, Piccolo, and himself. And they all got into it, and it took them across the lake without sail or oars.

"They reached the seashore without further adventures and sailed back to Musicland. On the way they passed the island of Zauberflöte, which was still trembling with lovely sound: but this time they knew better than to stop there. They went straight back to the City of Pleasant Sounds, to the palace of King Diapason, and they told him the whole story.

"The King was angry with Bourdon, and he sent his army, under the command of Tuba Mirabilis, who, helped by Posaune, Clarion, and Cymbal, captured Bourdon and his three brothers, Bass, Violone, and Ophicleide, and put them in prison in the Lake of Sighs. They are there to this day. And they are never allowed to go free in their own country, but they have to come to your world when some one has the gift; and that is why their voices are so gruff. Bassoon and Tromba were let off with a severe reprimand because they were sorry for what they had done. Then King Diapason ordered a great wedding to be held. And Lieblich Gedacht and Vox Angelica were married yesterday. It was the most gorgeous wedding ever seen. We were all of us there, and Unda Maris came from her home in the sea in a chariot drawn by sea-lions, and Echo came from her high castle in a chariot drawn by zephyrs. Tuba Mirabilis, Clarion, and the soldiers all wore their best armour and their brightest helmets.

"Vox Angelica's bridesmaids were the seven daughters of Echo, and her page was Piccolo. Lieblich Gedacht's best man was Waldhorn. And Voix Céleste, who is a nun, came from her convent to sing in the choir. Many of the fairies came to the wedding: Prince Myrtle was there, Cinderella, and the Marquis of Carrabas and his cat."

"And did Zauberflöte come?" asked Johan.

"No," said Quint, "she was not invited."

"And what happened to Hautboy, Cornet, and Viol d'Amore?" asked Johan.

"Well," said Quint, "they were all to have been married on the same day; but Muzette is very dainty and her wedding gown was not ready. It is being woven in Fairyland by the elves, and it is to be made of the petals of forget-me-nots and pinks, and her veil is to be spun out of dewdrops caught in the new moon. All this takes such a long time that the elves could not finish it by yesterday, so the King arranged that Hautboy and Clarabella, Viol d'Amore and Dolce, and Cornet and Muzette should be married in a month's time, all on the same day."

"At any rate," said Johan, "you will not miss that wedding. But where have Vox Angelica and Lieblich Gedacht gone to for their honeymoon?"

"They have gone to Lieblich Gedacht's cottage in the Woods of Melody, and they will live there for the rest of their lives; for all their lives will be one long honeymoon," said Quint. As he said this he climbed on to the manuals, and disappeared into the heart of the organ.

And Johan noticed that the sun had risen and that the sacristan was opening the cathedral for early Mass. A few minutes later Frantz walked up into the organ loft, and Johan asked him to draw the stops of Vox Angelica and Lieblich Gedacht together and alone. Frantz did this, and they blent their voices together in unison, and Johan understood that they were happier than they had ever been before.

THE VAGABOND

There was once upon a time a King and a Queen who had three daughters. The eldest was called Elsa, the second Elfrida, and the third Heartsease. All the fairies were invited to the christening of the two eldest daughters, and not one was left out. They came and showered gifts on the two babies, and promised them beauty, riches, prosperity, happiness, and long life. But when Heartsease was born, the King happened to be very busy drawing up a treaty with a neighbouring State, about the rights of preserving gold-fish in a certain pond which lay between the two kingdoms, so that when he invited the fairies to the christening he left out one of them: the Fairy of the Yellow Mines, who was wicked and powerful.

The other fairies came, and they said that Heartsease should be the kindest and the cleverest princess ever seen: her eyes should be as blue as forget-me-nots, her smile as bright as the morning, her hands as delicate as snowdrops, and her heart of pure gold. Moreover, she should sing like a lark, and ride wild horses, and do needlework better than all other princesses. Towards the end of the feast, the Fairy of the Yellow Mines arrived in a chariot drawn by two snorting dragons. She was all yellow, and her face was dry as a piece of parchment, and pinched and wrinkled with spite and envy.

"So it appears I am not worthy to be invited to this feast," she said. "I know I am old-fashioned, but in my time kings used to take the trouble to be civil to fairies. But since I have come unbidden I must not depart without bestowing a gift. Heartsease, in spite of her eyes the colour of forget-me-nots, in spite of her smile like the morning and her hands like snowdrops, shall not be pretty to look at, for her skin shall be marked with my special signature. And he who woos her will woo her for herself and for her heart, and not for her face."

So saying, the Fairy of the Yellow Mines chuckled, and flew away in her yellow chariot.

The King and the Queen were dreadfully vexed when this happened, and they at once asked Heartsease's godmother, who was none other than the Fairy of the Azure Lake, whether she could not do anything to help them.

"Alas! I cannot undo the mischief that has been done," she answered, "but nevertheless Heartsease shall be wooed and won, and her bridegroom shall be greater than that of her beautiful sisters." And when she had said this, the Fairy of the Azure Lake drove away in her chariot, which was made of honeysuckle, and driven by ten obedient bees.

Heartsease was the most beautiful little baby ever seen. Her hair was curly, her skin as soft as that of a rose-leaf, with many dimples in it, and her smile made those who looked at her happy the whole day long. Two years passed, and the King and the Queen began to think that the wicked fairy's words had only been a bad joke, when one day Heartsease began to cry, and it became clear that she was not well. She was put to bed, and the Court doctor was sent for. He looked at her, and said that the case was a very serious one. During a whole month little Heartsease was mortally sick, and she was given many nasty medicines which she drank without complaining. The King and the Queen never left her bedside day and night.

At last, at the end of the sixth week, the doctor said the turning-point had come, and that little Heartsease would get well. From that day onwards she began to recover, and in a month's time she was able to run about. But alas! her lovely soft skin had disappeared. It was pitted all over with deep marks, so that it appeared to be all shrivelled, and as yellow as the face of the Fairy of the Yellow Mines; and nobody could recognise in this dried-up, wizened face the lovely little child that had once been Heartsease. And in spite of her eyes, which were still as blue as forget-me-nots, and in spite of her smile, people could scarcely bear to look at her, poor little thing, such a fright had she become. And this, of course, was the doing of the Fairy of the Yellow Mines, who had cast a spell on Heartsease's face.

The King ordered all the looking-glasses in the house to be broken, lest Heartsease should catch sight of herself and be sad, and so she continued to play with her toys and ride on her white pony and be happy. But the King and the Queen were sad, because they loved Heartsease the best of all their daughters.

One day, when Heartsease was eight years old, she went out for a walk with her two sisters, and they met a vagabond in dark, tattered cloak who was playing a hurdy-gurdy, which is a thing like a big violin, with strings, and keys, and a handle at the end of it which you turn. The vagabond looked very poor and miserable, and he took off his cap and asked for a few pence, for he had not a penny to buy bread with.

Now Elsa and Elfrida, Heartsease's sisters, were very proud. They scowled at the vagabond, and told him to go about his business quickly, or else they would send for the soldiers and have him locked up in gaol. But Heartsease was sorry for him and said: "I cannot give you any money, because I have not got any, but take this: perhaps it will make you happy, because I love it very much, and talk to it when I am alone." And she took her favourite old doll which she always carried about with her, and gave it to him. It was not a pretty doll, and she had played with it so much that its clothes were frayed and torn; but it had a beautiful crown made of gold paper, and a necklace of large blue beads. And Heartsease loved it above all things, and it was her companion; because Elsa and Elfrida never let her play with them, for they said she was too small.

As soon as she had done this Elsa and Elfrida burst out laughing.

"Fancy giving a beggar a doll!" they said. "We should like to know what he can do with it!"

"Thank you kindly, little Princess," said the vagabond. "I shall never forget your kindness."

"A lot of good a beggar's kindness will do her," said Elsa.

"Perhaps he will bring her a bridegroom," said Elfrida.

"Perhaps he will wed her himself," said Elsa, and they both laughed.

"Nobody else will, for sure," said Elfrida.

The vagabond then turned to the two sisters and said—

"A day will come when you will envy your sister her bridegroom." And he hobbled away.

Elsa and Elfrida burst into a fit of laughter.

"Fancy," said Elsa, "our envying Heartsease!"

"Fancy," said Elfrida, "her ever having a bridegroom!"

Now Heartsease could not understand what they meant, for she did not know she was a fright; but their words made her thoughtful and sad, and she wondered what they were talking about. When she got home, she asked her father whether, when she grew up, she would find a bridegroom, and be married.

"Of course you will, dear little child," he said, and he took her on his knee, but she noticed that his eyes were filled with tears.

From that moment, Heartsease began to suspect that there was something wrong about herself, and that she was not quite the same as other children. One summer night, after she had been put to bed, her nurse and the nurserymaid were sitting by the nursery window darning some stockings. They thought Heartsease was asleep.

"Princess Elsa will be fifteen years old come Michaelmas," said the nurse.

"They'll be looking for a bridegroom for her soon," said the nurserymaid. "She's as tall as a grown-up lass already."

"I pity her husband," said the nurse; "she's a regular cross-patch she is, and as proud as a peacock."

"And as different from the little one as cloth from silk," said the nurserymaid.

"Ah!" sighed the nurse, "poor little lamb! they'll have a hard task to find her a suitor, although she deserves the best in the land."

Heartsease wondered what this could mean, and the more she pondered over it, the sadder she became.

The years passed by, and a great feast was held at Court to celebrate Princess Elsa's seventeenth birthday. All the princes of the land were invited, for the King and the Queen thought that the time had come for Elsa to be married. The three principal suitors were Prince Silvergilt, who possessed immense riches and countless jewels; King Sharpsword, who was a terrible fighter, and had slain two hundred knights in single combat; and Prince Simple Simon, who was the youngest son of a powerful king, and so simple that he was always laughed at by everybody. Besides these there were a number of less important knights and princes. As soon as the Prince Silvergilt set eyes on Princess Elsa, he made up his mind that she would make just the right wife for him, because she was beautiful and haughty, and he was determined that the queen of his country should be the proudest woman in the world, and should always be dressed in gold, and wear a heavy crown.

The King's feast was the most splendid that had ever been known, and it was followed by a display of fireworks and a ball. Prince Silvergilt danced with Princess Elsa, and King Sharpsword danced with Elfrida, and all the other princes and knights chose partners from among the crowd of beautiful princesses who were there; but nobody chose poor Heartsease, who sat lonely and very sad in a corner by herself.

At last, when the ball was nearly over, Prince Simple Simon noticed that Heartsease was all by herself, and he went up to her and asked her why she did not dance.

"Because," said Heartsease, "nobody has asked me to."

"Will you dance with me?" asked Simple Simon.

"Of course I will," said Heartsease, and he led her out. As he did this, Heartsease noticed that the courtiers looked at each other and hid a smile. They danced round the room; but Simple Simon was so awkward that although Heartsease, who danced like the wind, steered him beautifully, he kept on catching his sword in the trains of the princesses, and bumping up against them, so that all the courtiers tittered, although they tried to hide it, and Heartsease was obliged to ask him to go back to the quiet corner where she had been sitting.

"They are laughing because I dance so awkwardly," said Simple Simon. "Everybody laughs at me, except Lizbeth."

"Who is Lizbeth?" asked Heartsease.

"Lizbeth is the goose-girl in our village," he answered. "We are betrothed, and I am to wed her as soon as I have made my fortune."

"It was at me they were smiling," said Heartsease. "They always smile at me, and I do not know why. But perhaps you will tell me."

"I do not know," said Simple Simon.

"You see," said Heartsease, "the courtiers here pay me extravagant compliments. They tell me I am beautiful and clever; but I do not know whether it is true, because I have never seen my own face."

This was true, because there was no such thing as a looking-glass in the whole kingdom, and poor Heartsease had never been allowed to go near a river, a pond, a pool, or any place where she might have seen the reflection of her own face.

"I think," said Simple Simon, "your face is very beautiful. You have such nice, kind eyes. But then everybody says I am a bad judge. But haven't you ever looked at yourself in a mirror?"

"What is a mirror?" asked Heartsease.

"I will show you to-morrow morning," said Simple Simon.

At that moment a herald dressed in gold came into the ballroom, and blew a blast on his silver trumpet which meant that supper was ready. Heartsease would have liked to have gone in to supper with Simple Simon, but the Court etiquette did not allow it, and an old duke who was deaf came up, and gave her his arm.

The next morning Heartsease was feeding her tame birds in the garden when Simple Simon appeared before her.

"I have brought you a mirror," he said. And he gave her a piece of smooth polished steel which he had cut out of his own breastplate.

Heartsease looked at her face, and then two large tears ran down her cheeks.

"Oh!" she said, "it was unkind of you to mock me. I understand everything now. I see why nobody will speak to me. I am a hideous fright; my face is covered with spots and marks."

"But I wasn't mocking you," said Simple Simon. "I don't think those spots matter a bit. You have got such nice, kind eyes."

"No, no," said Heartsease, "I understand everything. Nobody will ever marry me."

"I am sure they will," said honest Simon; "why, I would have married you gladly myself if I had not been betrothed to Lizbeth." And so saying, Simple Simon said good-bye to Heartsease, for it was time for him to start once more on his travels.

Heartsease said good-bye to him and thanked him for his kindness, for she understood now that he had not meant to mock her, but that he spoke the truth, and she told him that she hoped he would make his fortune soon, and marry Lizbeth the goose-girl, and be happy ever afterwards.

When Simple Simon rode off on his old grey mare, Heartsease felt sad and lonely, for the only friend she had ever made was now leaving her for ever. The festivities went on all day long, because the Prince Silvergilt asked Elsa to be his wife, and it was settled that they should be married without any delay. So in the evening there was another great State ball, but Heartsease felt so sad at heart that she said she was not feeling well, and she went up to a little room where she kept her dolls, and all the treasures she had had when she was a child. This little room was in an attic in a side wing of the palace, and it looked over a narrow street, for the palace stood in the middle of the city. Heartsease had made this room a hiding-place for herself as soon as she was big enough to leave the nursery. Nobody knew it existed except her nurse, and she could go and play there when she wanted to be alone. She liked to look out on to the street and see the people coming and going, the horses and the carts clattering over the cobblestones, instead of on to the big empty gardens on which all the state-rooms looked out, and where you saw no one except the sentry walking up and down, and the courtiers, strutting about like peacocks in their wigs and hoops. The room had a little bed in it, and sometimes she slept there; but this evening she was not at all sleepy, and she leant out of her window and watched the evening star shining in the summer twilight, which was still tinged with yellow in the west.

Faintly in the distance she heard the sounds of harps, cymbals, and drums coming from the banqueting-hall, where the King was holding a feast. The little street beneath her was quite empty and silent, the curfew had sounded, and the watchman had blown his horn and told all good people to put out their lights and go to bed, and in the jutting-out casements of the pointed red-gabled houses opposite her, which seemed to lean over the street, there was not a light left.

Suddenly she heard the sound of footsteps tramping on the cobblestones, and round the corner of the street she saw a dark figure coming along, which seemed to her to be a man. It was dark now, and the sky was a deep and wonderful blue. The moon had not risen, and only a few stars twinkled, very large and bright.

The figure walked slowly along, keeping close to the walls of the houses opposite to her. When he was opposite the palace he stopped. She could not distinguish clearly who it was, but she saw at once it was a man. He was carrying something in his hand, and presently she became aware that it was a lute, or a musical instrument of some kind, for he began to play, and a thin thread of sound crept from the darkness and found a way straight into her heart.

Then it all at once came into her mind that she had seen this man before and heard these sounds already, and she remembered the vagabond who played a hurdy-gurdy, and to whom she had given her favourite doll, long ago when she was little. But now his music sounded different. "Perhaps," she thought, "it is because I am older and can understand it." However that may be, never in her life had she heard or imagined anything so melodious and so sweet. For while the vagabond played, he sang, and although the words of his song were in some tongue which was unknown to her, she seemed to understand every word of it. Although she had never heard the vagabond's voice before, it seemed familiar to her as if she had known it all her life. And there was something warm in it which gladdened you, and something soft and lovely like the tender colours of summer dawn. But more than all things Heartsease felt that the voice was the voice of a friend who would be kind to her and comfort her; and Heartsease felt she could listen to it for ever.

"Come away," it seemed to say, "from this palace and these unkind people, and I will give you freedom, and we will roam together over the wide world, and sleep beneath the stars, and drink of the clear brooks and bathe in the streams; in the summer the sky shall be our tent, and the stars shall be our candles, and in the winter we will make ourselves snug and warm in the heart of the woods; we will wander over hill and valley, and will float on a raft down the broad river till we come to the sea; and we will cross the great sea, and I will give you a little cottage of your own, all overgrown with honeysuckle, where the bees hum and boom, and there I will lull you to sleep with a song."

Then all at once the music ceased, and Heartsease wanted to call the minstrel, but he had vanished, and although he had sung quite loud, none of the people in the houses seemed to have noticed him.

All night long Heartsease dreamed of the vagabond and of his singing, and the next evening she waited at her window as soon as the sun set.

But the vagabond did not come that evening, nor the next evening either, and weeks and months went by but he did not come again.

A year after this Princess Elsa was married. The King and the Queen gave another great feast in honour of their second daughter, Elfrida, and this time King Sharpsword was betrothed to her, and the wedding was celebrated with pomp and ceremony. As usual there were feasting and dances every night, and although all the princes of the land were there, nobody took any notice of poor Heartsease except the old duke, who was obliged to lead her in to supper according to the etiquette of the Court. And this time Heartsease had no friend to talk to, for Simple Simon was not there, although she had news of him. He had made his fortune, much to everybody's surprise, by capturing a cruel ogre, and he had married Lizbeth the goose-girl, and they were as happy as the day is long. But although Heartsease was lonely and despised, she did not feel lonely any longer, for somewhere she felt she had a friend who would not forget her, and she remembered the marvellous song of the vagabond.

The night Elfrida was married, Heartsease again said she did not feel well, and she went to the little room in the attic, and waited by the window while the light faded from the twilight sky. And as soon as it grew dark, she heard the footsteps on the cobblestones, and soon the piercing notes of the sweet familiar voice echoed in the street, sighing, soothing, and binding her with a spell, healing her heartache and taking away her homesickness, and calling her away to the valleys and the hills. For hours she seemed to listen to the deep, deep tones, and then, as the year before, the sound suddenly ceased and the vagabond had vanished.

The next year Heartsease herself was seventeen years old, the age at which it was the custom for the royal princesses to be married. But although the King and the Queen made a great feast and invited all the princes of the land, not one of them asked the King for the hand of his daughter Heartsease, because they all thought it was impossible to marry a wife who was such a fright.

The King and the Queen were miserable, and they settled to wait another year, in case some kind prince might come who would be willing to marry Heartsease.

As for Heartsease, she begged her father and mother not to worry about her. She told them she did not want to marry any one, and that she was quite happy living at home and taking care of them. And they did not know that she had looked at herself in a mirror and had seen her face. But although she said this, and pretended to be happy and cheerful, she was really sad at heart because she was such a fright, and she was sure nobody could love her, and the only thing which consoled her was the mysterious vagabond who came once a year and sang beneath her window.

Soon after Heartsease's seventeenth birthday, her mother, the Queen, went one day for a ride in the forest by herself, and the wicked Fairy of the Yellow Mines carried her off in her chariot and locked her up in a castle. The people of the city searched for the Queen everywhere, but no trace of her was to be found, so that everybody thought she must have been eaten by wild beasts; but Heartsease knew this was not true, because she saw her mother in her dreams every night. Another year passed, and just before Heartsease's birthday came round, the old King married again. The new Queen was the godchild of the Fairy of the Yellow Mines. She was wicked, and owing to the spells which her godmother had taught her, she could make the King do anything she wished, and she made him believe the Queen had been eaten by wild beasts. No sooner were they married than her wickedness and her cruelty, which she had hidden up to that moment, became plain to everybody. She hated Heartsease, because Heartsease was good and unhappy, and she tormented her in every possible way; and to crown all, on the day before Heartsease's birthday, she said she could not have a lazy, good-for-nothing slut about the house, but that Heartsease must marry at once, and that since nobody would marry her of their own accord, she would find some one who should do so whether he liked it or not.

That very day the new Queen sent a message by a rat to her godmother, and the Fairy of the Yellow Mines arrived in her chariot drawn by two snorting dragons.

"It's about that child," said the Queen, when her godmother had arrived and settled herself comfortably in an arm-chair. "She bothers me. I want you to find her a husband—some one who will keep her in order and not stand any nonsense; at the same time I should like it to be a suitable and proper alliance—suitable for me too, that is to say."

"I quite understand," said the Fairy.

"You see," said the Queen, "the King won't live long, and when he dies I shall be Queen of the country, and I shall not want any of the King's sons-in-law to come bothering or interfering, disputing my right to the kingdom, or any nonsense of that kind. I am quite at my ease about Prince Silvergilt and King Sharpsword; they are so busy beating their wives that they will not bother me."

Now this was quite true, and Elfrida and Elsa were both of them unhappy; because their husbands were unkind, and they were obliged to wear stiff robes all day, and heavy crowns, and they were beaten if they did not look happy and cheerful.

"I have got the very thing," said the Fairy; "my dear nephew Crookedshanks is just what you want. He has been looking for a wife for a long time, but so far nobody has consented to marry him. He's so beautiful, you know"—and here the Fairy chuckled—"he's a dwarf and a hunchback, and he's got such a sweet, sweet temper. He'll keep the minx in order."

"But," said the Queen, "I hope he won't interfere with me."

"Never fear," said the Fairy, "he lives inside the copper mountain, deep down underground, like a mole among the gnomes, and he would not leave the treasures he hoards there for all the kingdoms of the earth."

Thus it was settled that Heartsease should marry Crookedshanks, and the Fairy of the Yellow Mines brought him to the palace the next day, which was Heartsease's birthday.

Crookedshanks was hideous to look at, and he was as spiteful as he was ugly. And when Heartsease was brought to him, and told that this was to be her husband, she could not believe her eyes. She begged her father to save her; but her father was now so completely spellbound by the wicked Queen that he could not do anything, and so all preparations were made for Heartsease's wedding, which was to take place on the morrow.

But in the evening, just before the feast began, Heartsease escaped from the banqueting-hall when no one was looking, and ran up to the little room in the attic. Then she opened the windows wide and leaned out into the street.

It was a lovely evening. There was a smell of sun-dried hay in the air, and the dust of the town made a golden cloud in the west which faded presently, and when the evening star lit its lamp the sky was soft and blue. In the palace everybody was looking for Heartsease. They were searching the halls and the gardens, but nobody thought of looking for her in that out-of-the-way attic, except her nurse, but she did not tell anybody. Presently Heartsease heard the well-known footstep of the vagabond, and her heart gave a great leap for joy.

He walked right up to the house opposite her window, and began to sing. And this time his beautiful voice was louder and stronger than it had ever been. And Heartsease leant out of the window and cried out—

"Come, for I have heard and I am ready!"

The song ceased, but this time the vagabond did not vanish. He crossed the narrow street, and entered at one of the side doors of the palace which was just beneath Heartsease's window. Heartsease heard him walking up the winding wooden stairway, and soon the vagabond entered her room and stood before her in his rags and tatters, poor, pale, ill-kempt, limping and miserable. And Heartsease ran to him and cried out—

"At last you have come, my lover, my lord and my bridegroom!"

"Do you really wish to come with me?" he asked. "My kingdom is the open field, and my palaces are the dark wood and the highway; my brothers and sisters are the cold winds, the rain, the snow, and the hail; my jewels are tears, and my wealth is sorrow."

And Heartsease said: "I will come with you to your kingdom and dwell in your palaces; and your brothers and sisters shall be my brothers and sisters, and I will wear your jewels and share your wealth as long as I live!"

The vagabond gave Heartsease a silver penny, which was all his wealth, and they climbed down the narrow staircase and went out into the night.

In the King's palace on the night of the banquet there was great commotion because Heartsease could not be found anywhere. The courtiers searched high and low, in the palace and in the gardens, but all in vain, until at last they gave it up and the banquet was begun without her.

The Queen was angry, and the old King was sad, and Crookedshanks gnashed his teeth and pinched everything he met, out of spite. The next morning the nurse came to the King and told him Heartsease could not be found anywhere. So the King issued a proclamation which was sent far and wide over the whole kingdom, saying that whoever should find his daughter Heartsease would receive half of his kingdom. But although a great number of people set out to try and find Heartsease, they none of them succeeded, and most of them gave up the quest after a time.

Now Heartsease and the vagabond wandered far over hill and dale, north and south, east and west, earning their bread by songs, until they came to the grim castle in which Heartsease's mother had been imprisoned by the wicked fairy.

The vagabond sang a song outside the castle, so that Heartsease's mother could hear him, and he told her that Heartsease was alive and had not forgotten her, and that one day the wicked fairy's spell would be broken. And Heartsease saw her mother's hand waving through the thick bars of the narrow window of the castle. Then they wandered on till they came to the kingdom of King Silvergilt, and there, in a castle, were Prince Silvergilt and his wife Elsa; and King Sharpsword and his wife Elfrida were staying with him. Elsa and Elfrida were both of them unhappy because their husbands were so unkind.

The vagabond and Heartsease went under Elfrida's window, and the vagabond sang a song, but no sooner had he begun than Prince Silvergilt sent out his soldiers, and told them to drive the vagabonds away. Now Elsa and Elfrida were sad and sorry because the vagabond's song had made them feel happier, but they dared not say a word. Only when it grew dark they crept out of the castle, into the wood, which was next to it, to see if they could find the two vagabonds and give them alms. They wandered about in the forest, and they soon came to a little hut where the vagabond and Heartsease were lying fast asleep on a heap of leaves.

"Here they are, poor, poor people!" said Elsa; "they have got nothing to eat."

"They must be very cold," said Elfrida, and she took off her cloak and laid it over them.

"Do you remember a vagabond telling us we should one day envy Heartsease her husband?" said Elsa.

"Poor Heartsease, she'll never have a husband; but I'm sure we envy her now, wherever she is," said Elfrida.

"I would give worlds to see her again," said Elsa. "Poor, poor Heartsease, to think how unkind we were to her!" And Elsa and Elfrida began to cry bitterly, and their tears fell upon Heartease's face.

Then leaving behind them some bread and wine which they had brought with them, and a purse full of gold, and their cloaks, they went back to the castle; neither of them had recognised Heartsease.

The next morning when the vagabond and Heartsease rose, they found the gifts that the sisters had brought, and the vagabond told Heartsease to go and look at herself in a pool which was hard by. When Heartsease looked into the pool she gave a cry of surprise, because the ugly marks had gone from her face, and she looked like what she had been when she was a little girl—lovely, and fresh as a rose in the morning dew, and the loveliest princess in the world.

"Now," said the vagabond, "we will go to your father's castle."

So they started for the King's castle, but it was far off, and they had to pass through many cities and villages; and when the people in the cities and the villages heard the vagabond singing in the street, and saw Heartsease, they wondered at her great beauty, and when the vagabond sang they were afraid, and they thought he must be a wizard and that Heartsease was a witch, and they often drove them away from their doors; so that Heartsease and the vagabond with difficulty earned enough bread to keep them alive.

At last they reached the city of the King, and there they read the King's proclamation, which said that whoever should find Heartsease would receive half the kingdom. The vagabond went straight to the King's palace, and asked to see the King; but the soldiers stopped him at the gate and said that beggars were not allowed to go into the palace. But when the vagabond said he had found Princess Heartsease they durst not forbid him to enter. So the vagabond was led to the King, and he told him that he had found his daughter.

The King was overjoyed, but Heartsease's stepmother said it was not true, and the King told the vagabond to bring Heartsease to the palace. He went to fetch her, and when he brought her to the palace everybody was dazzled by her beauty, but nobody recognised her, not even the King, for he could not understand how the Heartsease whom he remembered could have turned into such a vision of beauty. But there were two people in the castle who said that they recognised her: one was her old nurse, and the other was Simple Simon, who happened to be there. Simple Simon said he saw no difference in her at all: that she was now just as she had always been, with the same kind eyes and lovely smile. And when he said this, the whole Court laughed, and they said that Simple Simon would never cease to be a ninny. And as for the nurse, the Queen said she must be locked up in the dungeon at once for telling lies. Then the wicked Queen said that the vagabond was a wizard, and that Heartsease was a witch, and that they had killed the real Heartsease, and that they must both be burnt alive in the public square. And owing to her magic everybody believed this, and the vagabond and Heartsease were thrown into prison.

But the King, who did not want them to be burnt, sent for his daughters Elsa and Elfrida, to see if they recognised Heartsease. Elfrida and Elsa arrived with their husbands, and Heartsease was brought before them, but she was not allowed to speak; and owing to the wicked Queen's spells, neither Elfrida nor Elsa recognised their sister. After this it was settled that the vagabond and Heartsease should be burnt in the public square.

On the day this was to happen the whole town gathered together to see the wizard; and the vagabond and Heartsease were driven from the prison to the square, where a large pile of fagots had been prepared, in a cart. And when the people saw Heartsease, a wave of pity went through the crowd, so lovely and so innocent was her face. The King and the Queen, his daughters, and all the Court were there, and when the vagabond got out of the cart he asked the King to grant him one last favour: and this was to allow him to sing a song before he died. And the King granted it him.

The vagabond began to sing, and he sang the sweetest and most wonderful song that had ever been heard; he sang of the love that never dies, and the love which is stronger than death; and as he sang, the evil spells of the wicked Queen died in the King's heart, and he remembered his true wife, and the great love he bore her; and Elsa and Elfrida recognised the voice, and they cried out—

"It is the vagabond we heard when we were children, and it is Heartsease after all!"

And the King cried out: "Yes, it is Heartsease after all!" And he ran to her, and took her in his arms, and covered her with kisses. Then he said to the vagabond: "You have brought me back my daughter. You shall be my son and you shall have half my kingdom."

But the wicked Queen said: "That is impossible! How can you give half your kingdom to a vagabond in rags and tatters?"

But the King said: "I do not care if he is a vagabond or not. He shall wed my daughter and have half my kingdom."

And as he said this the vagabond threw off his dark, tattered cloak, and there stood before the throng a wonderful shining figure with wings, and golden hair, and across his shoulder there was slung a silver bow with a quiver full of silver arrows, and he held a lyre in his hand, and all round him was a cloud of golden light like the fire of sunrise. And his face shone, and his eyes were like stars. But when the wicked Queen saw this, she was so angry that she burst with rage, and all her spells were undone.

At the very same moment the Fairy of the Azure Lake arrived in her chariot of honeysuckle drawn by ten bees, and she brought Heartsease's mother with her, and Heartsease's old nurse, whom she had released from prison. You can imagine their surprise, and how they all cried for joy! and how happy they all were!

Then the King said to the vagabond: "You shall wed Heartsease and receive half my kingdom; but who are you, noble prince, and what is your name?"

And the vagabond answered: "I will wed Heartsease, but I have a kingdom of my own, and we must live there and nowhere else; and as for my name, it is Love, the Vagabond, but now I shall wander no more."

Then Crookedshanks was banished from the Court, and the Fairy of the Azure Lake changed Prince Silvergilt into a candlestick, and King Sharpsword into a grindstone, and she found two kind new husbands for Elsa and Elfrida. And a great wedding was held, and the day after it Love the Vagabond put Heartsease on a snow-white steed, and they started for the kingdom of Love the Vagabond, and they galloped across the plains, down the valleys, and over the hills until they came to the sea, which is at the end of the world, and they rode over the sea as easily as if it had been a grassy meadow.

And on the other side of the sea they came to a country of blue hills and green woods and golden cornfields, and there in a garden full of roses was a little cottage covered with honeysuckle, round which the bees hummed and boomed.

"This," said the Vagabond, "is my kingdom. Here is our home where we shall live happily together."

And Heartsease and the Vagabond lived happily in this little cottage for ever afterwards; and the King and Queen, and their sisters, and Simple Simon and Lizbeth his wife, often paid them long visits.

THE MINSTREL

Once upon a time, in a small village in the mountains, there lived a blacksmith and his wife. They were poor but they were happy; the blacksmith had always plenty of work, and their only sorrow was that they had no children.

One day the blacksmith's wife walked from the village down into the valley to a farmhouse to buy some eggs from the farmer, whom she knew. On her way back, as it was a fine spring day and the snows had melted, she loitered on the mountain so as to gather some wild-flowers.

As she was picking the flowers she heard some one muttering behind her, and turning round, she saw an old woman, bent and worn, who was muttering a supplication.

"What can I do for you?" asked the blacksmith's wife.

"Give me the eggs you have in that basket," said the old woman.

The blacksmith's wife, although she was afraid she would be scolded at home, durst not refuse, and gave the eggs to the old woman.

"Thank you kindly," said the old woman; "in return for your kindness I will grant you a wish."

The blacksmith's wife at once answered: "I wish to have a daughter who shall be more beautiful than the Queen's daughter."

"Your wish shall be granted," said the old woman. "But take this charm, hang it up over your hearth, and never give it away, for if you do, you will give your daughter with it."

So saying the old woman gave the blacksmith's wife a small copper coin made in the shape of a heart, and as soon as she had done this she hobbled off into the wood.

The blacksmith's wife went home and told her husband about her adventure, and they hung the copper coin over their hearth and they laughed for joy.

As the fairy had predicted, a daughter was born to them, and she grew to be such a lovely little child that the blacksmith and his wife were almost frightened. She was more like a fairy than a mortal. It seemed as if she had invisible wings; her skin was more delicate than a pearly sea-shell, and one expected to see little elves dancing round her when she played in the fields.

They had christened her Snowflower, because she was like the flowers that grew on the great mountains. And the name was a proper one, for she loved the snow-fields and the spaces of the great hills. Everybody who saw her was amazed—some said that she would wed the King's son; others that she would one day be the Empress of the West; but one old crone, who was spiteful, said that she was much too beautiful to live long.

One day when Snowflower was nine years old, her father and her mother had gone up into the hills to visit some friends. It was Saturday afternoon, and they had left Snowflower in charge of the shop, and had said that they would not be back till late. Snowflower was sitting outside in the street, watching the sunset—it was a warm summer's eve—when she heard some one singing a strange song.

Never had she heard anything so strange and so beautiful before: the voice was a man's voice, deep and hoarse, and it seemed to come from very far away; the song he sang was soft and sad, but it had a piercing note in it, something that made you listen whether you wished to or no; it was a voice which you felt must be obeyed.

Snowflower was lost in dreams, and when the singing stopped, she would have given worlds and worlds for it to begin again. While she was wondering who the singer could be, she suddenly became aware of a shadow across the street, and she saw before her a tall minstrel carrying a lute. His face was half muffled in a black cloak; and all that she could see distinctly were two dark eyes, very sad, but bright as stars. The sun had set, the stars were coming out, and Snowflower was afraid. Nevertheless she at once asked him whether it was he who had been singing. He said—

"Yes, it was I."

"Shall I ever hear you again?" asked Snowflower.

"Yes, if you will give me a reward," said the minstrel.

"What can I give you?" asked Snowflower. "I have no money, and my father and my mother have gone to the farm and they won't be back till late."

"All I want," said the minstrel, "is the little copper coin in the shape of a heart that hangs over your hearth."

"Oh! you may have that with pleasure," said Snowflower, "it is only a brass farthing." And she ran indoors, and fetched it, and gave it to him. "Only now you must sing to me again," she said.

"I promise to sing to you again, but not now," said the minstrel, and he walked away into the darkness.

When Snowflower's father and mother came home, they noticed at once that the little copper coin had gone, and Snowflower told them that she had given it to a wandering minstrel.

Her mother was vexed and cried; but her father said—

"Never mind, never mind, no harm ever came yet of giving alms to the poor."

The years passed by, and Snowflower never once saw the mysterious minstrel again, and she soon forgot all about him. She grew up into a most beautiful maiden; and when she was seventeen, there was no one to compare with her in the whole country. She was dazzling like the snow on the mountains, and soft as the blush that steals over them in the dawn, and her eyes were like the pools that reflect the sky in the hidden places of the hills. So beautiful was she that the fame of her spread far and wide, and the King thought that she would make an excellent wife for his only son, who was just old enough to marry.

So he sent one of his courtiers in disguise to the village in the mountains; he was to find out whether what the people said about Snowflower was true or not.

He came to the village and saw Snowflower, and when he returned to the palace once more, he told the king that Snowflower was far more beautiful than what men told of her, and that it was indeed impossible to describe her, for she was more beautiful than all mortals, but like a fairy or a dream-child. When the King heard this, he set out with many of his courtiers for the village in the hills, and they found Snowflower sitting and spinning at the door of the blacksmith's shop.

The blacksmith and his wife were astonished and frightened when they saw all these grand folk coming to their home, and when the King said that he wished his son to marry their daughter they could hardly speak for surprise. The King's son was as fine and as brave a lad as any in the land, but it was settled that he was not to marry till he was twenty-one, and now he was only twenty. So the King said he would come back in a year's time and fetch Snowflower.

The blacksmith was of course delighted at his good fortune; but Snowflower said that she did not wish to leave her native village, and her father's home, and that she was quite happy where she was. And her mother, remembering what the fairy had said, and how Snowflower had given away the copper coin, was frightened, and she and Snowflower cried bitterly together. But the blacksmith said this was nonsense, and laughed at the two women for being so silly.

After a year had gone by, the King sent a whole train of courtiers to fetch Snowflower, and they put her on a pony and they brought her to the city and the palace of the King.

It was arranged that the wedding should be held a few days after her arrival.

Snowflower was given a gorgeous room in the palace looking out on to a wide courtyard, round which there were statues and colonnades; and splendid preparations were made for her wedding ceremony.

She was introduced to the Prince directly, and he fell in love with her at first sight. As for Snowflower, she knew not whether she loved the Prince or not, but she thought she had never seen so charming and handsome a person before, and she would have been quite happy but for a home-sickness which never left her, for she longed for the sight of the snowy mountains, the green valleys, and the little village where she was born; and she felt that she could not live for ever far away from the snows, and the streams, and the flowers of the great white hills.

She had gone to bed early and fallen asleep at once, but towards midnight she was awakened by a sound which seemed to be familiar to her; she ran to the window and looked out into the courtyard, whose pillars were gleaming in the moonlight. Again she heard a sound, and then on the midnight wind there were borne into the room the notes of a song which she thought she had heard once before, long ago, in her home in the hills. It was a hoarse voice, which seemed to come from far away; a mournful voice and sweet, but in spite of its sweetness there was a strange spell in it and something which called for and demanded submission. She listened, and now, although she knew she had heard it before, she could not tell when or where; it was different from anything she remembered, and more beautiful; and yet, as she listened, her heart beat fast, and she knew not whether it was the voice of a friend or an avenging foe who was singing that hoarse serenade.

She withdrew from the window in fright, but the song grew louder; it called her with sound like that of bugles on a field of battle in the evening when the fight is ended—silvery, manful, and triumphant.

And then her heart beat faster than ever, for she knew that the voice was that of a lover; and she knew that she could not resist his song.

And she looked once more out of the window, and there in the courtyard, dark against one of the gleaming pillars, she saw a tall man muffled in a black cloak, a man whom she recognised. She ran back from the casement and called out in a great terror, but nobody answered her call.

Then across the cobblestones of the yard she heard the tramp of loud footsteps, as though a knight in armour were walking across it; and presently she heard the same heavy tramp on the wide marble steps that led up to her room. Nearer and nearer they came, till she heard a rap like that of a great sword against her door. He knocked so loudly that the noise was like thunder, and yet no one in the palace seemed to be disturbed. She tried to call out once more, but her voice died away in her throat; she tried to run, but she remained motionless.

Then the door was opened wide. And there entered, muffled in a dark cloak so that you could only see his eyes, the minstrel to whom she had given the heart-shaped copper coin that used to hang over her father's hearth. And then all at once she knew that the minstrel was not a foe but a friend, and she stretched out her hand and grasped his hand.

As soon as she did this he threw aside his cloak, and there stood before her a wonderful knight in armour, whose face was bright as snow and whose eyes were like stars. And he took her in his arms and carried her down the broad steps into the courtyard, and there a horse was waiting, and he mounted it and set Snowflower in front of him, and they galloped away through the gates, through the city, and over the plains beyond.

The next day Snowflower could not be found anywhere, and although the whole kingdom was searched far and wide, no trace of her was discovered.

When Snowflower went away from her village, the blacksmith's wife was very sad, although Snowflower had promised to visit her often. But when she woke up on the morning that Snowflower should have wedded the Prince, she was astonished to see that the little copper coin was hanging once more over their hearth, and she felt quite happy once more; for she knew now, although she could not tell why, that all was well with Snowflower.

THE HUNCHBACK, THE POOL AND THE MAGIC RING

There was once upon a time a King and a Queen who had three sons. The two eldest were big and strong, but the third was a cripple and a hunchback, because a wicked fairy, whom the Queen had forgotten to invite to his christening, had cast a spell over him in his cradle. Yet the King and the Queen loved their third son best of all, and this made his brothers jealous. When the three brothers were grown up, the King fell sick, and he knew that he was going to die. And so he called his three sons to him on his deathbed.

"Now that you are big and strong," he said to the two eldest, "it is time you went out into the world to seek your fortune. I will give to each of you a good horse, a suit of armour, a bag of gold, and a sharp sword; and to you," he said to the youngest, "I will give this castle, because you are not strong enough to go and seek your fortune for yourself. So you shall stay at home and look after your mother."

And soon after he had said this he died.

Now the two eldest brothers were very angry because the hunchback had been given the castle, and they said to each other: "Our father was old and feeble and did not know what he was doing: we will not give our brother the castle. Indeed, it would be of no use to him, but we will keep it for ourselves, and we will get rid of him, because it is a disgrace to have a hunchback in the family."

So they told their mother that they were going to take their brother with them, to show him the world, and they promised to look after him carefully. They started the next day, early in the morning, and when they had reached a large forest, they told the hunchback that he must seek his fortune by himself, and they took away his horse from him and his sword and his cloak. And the next day they rode home to the castle and said that their brother had been eaten by a bear in the night, entirely owing to his own fault.

When the young prince was left to himself, he was very sad, and did not know what to do, and he sat down by the side of a pool and cried bitterly. As he was crying, he heard a voice coming out of the pool and asking him what was the matter.

"I am crying," he said, "because I am a hunchback and I have been deserted by my two brothers," and he told all his story. Then he heard the voice laugh softly and say that everything could be put to rights. "Look into the pool," said the voice, "and tell me what you see at the bottom of it."

The hunchback looked, and said that he saw a gold ring.

"You must pull out the gold ring and put it on your finger," said the voice.

The hunchback thrust his arm into the pool and pulled out a gold ring, and no sooner had he put it on his finger than a beautiful woman stood in front of him. She had golden hair which fell to her feet, and large, soft eyes, and he thought she must be a fairy. And so she was: but she had been imprisoned in the pool by the same wicked fairy who had not been invited to the christening of the young Prince.

"You have done me a great service," said the fairy, "and I will not be ungrateful. Look into the pool."

The hunchback looked into the pool and saw his own reflection. But something wonderful had happened, for he was no longer hunchbacked, but far taller and stronger than his brothers, and the handsomest and most gallant-looking young Prince that the world had ever seen.

"Now," said the fairy, "all will be well with you. You have only to go into the world and you will make your fortune; but you must remember carefully what I tell you now. You must not lose the ring which I have given you, and never take it off your finger; and above all things you must never put it back into the pool. For whenever you take it off your finger, you will become a hunchback once more, and if you put it back into the pool, you will remain a hunchback for ever." And so saying the fairy disappeared.

Then the hunchback walked through the forest, whistling for joy; and at sunset he reached a large town. As soon as he reached the town, a large coach drawn by six cream-coloured horses passed him, and in the coach was a beautiful Princess, driving with her father, who was King of the country. Directly she caught sight of the Prince she stopped the coach and begged him to get in, and they drove to the palace. "At last," she said to her father, "I have found a man whom I will consent to marry."

And when the King, her father, learnt who the stranger was, he was very pleased, and offered him the hand of his daughter. And the Prince learned that from far and wide suitors had come to seek the hand of the Princess, but she had never been willing to look at any of them. And as the King was anxious that his daughter should marry, because she had a bad temper, he was very pleased at what had happened.

The Prince consented readily enough to marry so beautiful a Princess; but when they were left alone he told her all his story. The Princess did not believe it, and so as to prove the truth of his words he took off his ring, and he stood before her in his true shape, a cripple and a hunchback.

The Princess screamed and burst into a flood of tears, and abused the poor Prince, and although he had put the ring on again and resumed his splendid shape, she bade him begone out of her sight for ever. "For how could I marry a man," she said, "who might turn into a monster if he happened to lose a ring?"

So the Prince went away with a heavy heart, and started on his travels once more. He travelled far, and visited many cities, and wherever he went he was received with the greatest favour; for no one had ever seen so handsome a Prince, and many kings offered him their daughters in marriage. But the Prince turned a deaf ear now to their offers, and he was sad at heart, for he felt that the magic gift which he had received brought him no happiness, and he knew that he was wearing a mask and deceiving himself and the whole world.

Now it happened that one day during his travels he reached the seashore, and as darkness was falling he asked for shelter from a fisherman who had a hut on the beach. The fisherman bade him welcome, and told his wife to bring him some porridge. And as he sat eating his supper the fisherman's daughter worked at her spinning-wheel in the corner of the room, and sang a song which was like this:—

"He brought me silver, he brought me gold,
I bade him go his way;
My heart was bought and my heart was sold
Upon a summer's day.

He brought me horses and banners bold,
I bade him go his way;
My heart was bought and my heart was sold
Upon a summer's day.

For a sigh, a song, and a tale half-told,
And for a wisp of hay,
My heart was bought and my heart was sold
Upon a summer's day."

He looked at the fisherman's daughter. Her eyes were blue as the sky, and her cheeks were fresh as the salt sea. He looked at her and he fell in love with her at first sight. And she blushed and looked down, and although neither of them had spoken a word, they both knew that they would love each other for ever and ever.

The next day the Prince said good-bye to the fisherman's daughter, and when he said good-bye her eyes filled with tears so that it hurt him to go away. The sun was shining on the sea and a fresh breeze was blowing, and many white sails were scudding in the distance through the foam, and something stirred and leapt in the Prince's heart, and before he knew what he had done, he said: "I love you, and I shall always love you, and I am going away."

"Take me with you," said the fisherman's daughter, and the Prince smiled and lifted the fisherman's daughter on to his saddle, and they galloped away into the morning. They rode on and on, but the

Prince guided his horse to a dark forest. The thick grass underneath them was wet with dew, and the bushes and the undergrowth glistened in the sunlight. The blackbird was whistling, and the finches answered him from the oak-trees, and far away the cuckoo called over and over again.

Soon they reached a dark pool. Up to now the Prince had not spoken a word. He got off his horse and lifted the fisherman's daughter, who was as light as a feather, on to the ground.

"Now," he said, "I have got a sad tale to tell you. I am not really what you think I am. I am not a handsome Prince, but only a poor crippled hunchback, so ugly that people hate to look at me."

"What does it matter?" said the fisherman's daughter. "I would love you whether you were a hunchback or not. Perhaps I should love you even more."

"We will see," he said; "at any rate I have made up my mind to be what I am for ever and not to deceive people any more." And he threw his ring into the pool.

Then a soft moan was heard in the forest, and the birds flew away from their nests. The Prince stood before the fisherman's daughter in his true shape: a hunchback and a cripple. He was so sad that he cried bitterly, just as he had done on the day when his brothers had deserted him.

The fisherman's daughter cried too, to see that he was sad; but she kissed away his tears, and she told him that she loved him more than ever, and he knew by the sound of her voice that it was true.

Then he heard a voice coming from the pool, which said: "Look into the pool."

And they both looked and saw the reflection of the Prince. The hunchback had gone, and he was big, handsome, and strong, and just as he had been when the fisherman's daughter had first seen him. And then they both laughed, and kissed each other over and over again. The Prince had regained his splendid shape, which he was never to lose again; and he put the fisherman's daughter on his horse, and they rode home to the castle where he had been born, and they found his mother looking out of the window in case he should come back that day; and they were married the next morning in great pomp, and his two brothers came back—everything had fared ill with them, and they were poor and miserable—and he forgave them, and the Prince and the fisherman's daughter lived happily for ever afterwards.

THE SILVER MOUNTAIN

There was once upon a time a King who lived in a golden palace on the top of a high hill. He was powerful, wise, and good; his reign had been a scroll of glory, and he had scattered happiness and plenty on the people of his kingdom. The King had three sons, and when he felt that his death was approaching, he grew troubled in his mind as to which of them should inherit his kingdom. In his country it had been the everlasting custom for the King to leave his kingdom not to his eldest son, but to that one of his family whom he considered to be fittest to rule.

Now the King's eldest son was a soldier, a fine lad and a brave man; indeed, he was said to be the strongest and bravest youth in the land. The second son was a scholar; from his earliest youth he had pored over books, and he remembered what was in them even after he had finished reading them; he knew all about the habits of animals, and he looked at the stars through a long telescope of his own invention. The third son was a fool.

The King was perplexed as to which of these three should inherit his kingdom, for he reasoned thus: "My eldest son is too wild, my second son is too clever, and my third son is too foolish." So the King thought the best thing he could do would be to consult his Fairy Godmother, and he wrote her a long letter explaining the difficulty.

His Fairy Godmother answered his letter directly. She said she was sorry she could not come and see him, but that she was kept indoors by a bad cold. She quite understood the difficulty of the choice, but she advised the King to send his sons to look for the Silver Mountain, and to leave his kingdom to him who should find it.

The King said to himself, as soon as he had read this letter: "Of course; how extremely stupid of me not to have thought of this before!" So he sent for his sons, and he said: "To-morrow morning I wish all three of you to start and to look for the Silver Mountain, and I will leave my kingdom to him who finds it."

Early the next morning the three youths—they were all grown up—started on their search. The eldest son took his swiftest horse and went off at a gallop. He had not gone very far before he met a man who was also riding on a swift horse in the same direction. He asked him where he was going, and the second man said he was looking for the Silver Mountain, as he had heard that the man who found it should inherit a rich kingdom.

"That is true," said the King's son, "nevertheless the quest is not for you; it is only the sons of the King who are entitled to take part in this quest."

"But," said the stranger, "I intend to fight the King's sons and to kill them; then I shall find the mountain and inherit the kingdom."

"We shall see about that," said the King's son; and he proposed that they should fight then and there, which they did, and the King's son was victorious. He overcame the stranger and killed him, and leaving the body to be picked by the crows, he went on his way.

After many days, he came to a large town where the palace and chief buildings were all draped in black, and the people of the place were walking about with sad faces, talking in whispers. He asked some one what was the cause of all this grief, and he was told that the chief man of the country, who some time ago had set out upon some fantastic quest, had been killed by a robber in the woods, and that it was only now his bones had been brought home.

"It is for this reason we are sad," said the man, "for we are without a king."

On hearing this the King's son said: "There is no cause for grief. I will be your king." And he rode straight to the palace, and dismounting from his horse walked up the steps of the throne and placed the crown upon his head, and nobody durst say him nay.

Then the King's son thought to himself: "I have now solved the whole matter. It is needless for me to search all over the world for a Silver Mountain which I possibly may never find at all, or which my brothers may find sooner than I do, in order to inherit a kingdom, when I can thus gain almost as good a kingdom without any trouble at all."

So he thought no more about the Silver Mountain, or of his father, or of his ancient home, but he remained in this foreign country and married a wife, and ruled over it, and he lived in splendour and plenty.

The first thing which the second son did when he started on his quest was to consult an old scholar who lived in a hermitage, and who was famous for being the most learned man in the whole world. The King's second son went to him and said: "I want to find the Silver Mountain in order that I may inherit my father's kingdom."

The scholar said to him: "It is a good thing that you came to me for advice. Nobody in the world can help you as well as I can. There is no such thing as the Silver Mountain, and I daresay you know that already; nevertheless your father was a wise man to have made this quest the condition of the inheritance."

"But," said the King's son, "if there is no such thing as the Silver Mountain, there remains nothing for me to do but to go home and claim my inheritance."

"Not at all," said the old man. "It is of no avail to say that there is no such thing as the Silver Mountain, especially when almost everybody in the world is quite certain that the thing exists. Where your task lies is to find out what people think is the Silver Mountain, and to prove to them that it is not silver at all, but an ordinary mountain just like any other. That is what you must do." And so saying the old man refused to discuss the matter any further.

So the King's son set out on his quest once more, and on the way he met many people who were all seeking for the Silver Mountain. They were all anxious to find it, because they said that the man who found it would be a great king; and the King's son asked them to guide him to the place where it was likely to be. This they were willing to do, and after they had journeyed for many days, through forests and swamps, across large rivers, down steep valleys, and over wooded hills, they reached a wide plain; and beyond this plain rose a great chain of mountains, and in the centre of this chain there towered one mountain higher than the rest, and it was covered with clouds.

The people pointed to this mountain and said: "Without doubt, that is the Silver Mountain."

The King's son said he would climb this mountain, and he took the people with him. The ascent was steep and perilous, and many a time those who were with him would have turned back, had he not encouraged them and led them on by his fiery words, and after many days of toil and hardship, they reached the summit of the mountain, whence they obtained a view over the whole country.

Then the King's son said to them: "This is the highest mountain in the whole of the land—the whole of the land is now revealed to us. We know all there is to be known about this country, and it is quite plain that this mountain is a mountain just like any other, and that in the whole world there is no such thing as a Silver Mountain; therefore we will now go back and tell this to the whole world, and save our friends and our brothers from wasting their time and exhausting themselves in fruitless labour over an insane quest."

So they went back to the country, and announced the news far and wide that there was no such thing as a Silver Mountain, and that those who had set out on the quest of it had better return to their homes.

Now when the people heard this they were angry, and they threw stones at the King's son, and he was compelled to flee from their city and to seek shelter in the old scholar's home. But from that time forward many people in the country ceased to think of the Silver Mountain any more, or to search for it, and even among those who were angry with the King's son there were many who felt that his words were true nevertheless.

The third son started also on the quest. He sought out all the highest mountains of the country, and convinced himself that none of them could be the Silver Mountain, and yet he was sure there was such a thing somewhere, and he persisted in believing this, and in saying it. He spent many years of fruitless search, but he never gave up the quest, nor did he ever lose hope that one day he should accomplish it.

One evening, after he had been searching all day, he lay down, footsore and weary, and he said to himself aloud: "If only the fairies would help me, I should find the mountain soon enough."

No sooner had he said this than a beautiful fairy stood before him and said: "I will help you to find the Silver Mountain," and she gave him a small mirror made of polished steel, whereupon she immediately vanished.

The King's youngest son took the mirror and looked into it, and there he saw very distinctly the image of his father lying ill, propped up by pillows, dying and lonely, without any of his children about him. And the King's youngest son said to himself—

"What does it matter to me whether I inherit the kingdom or not? Before I think of that I must go back and see my father before he dies. I would much rather my brothers found the mountain before me, and inherited the kingdom, than that my father should die without my saying 'Good-bye' to him."

And he turned back, and made for his home as quickly as possible.

Now the King's palace was on the top of a high hill, and the King's youngest son approached it from the back, where he had never been before in his life, and towards evening he emerged from the forest and saw this hill before him, shining in the sunset, with the King's golden palace at the summit of it; and in the clear glory of the sunset the hill shone like silver, and the King's youngest son, as he looked at it, said—

"Why, this is the Silver Mountain!" And as he ran up the hill as fast as he could he saw that it was of silver after all. So he rushed into his father's bedroom, crying: "Father, I have found the Silver Mountain—it was here the whole time—at home—and we have all lived on the top of it without knowing it!"

The King was very pleased to see his son, and he said: "My son, what you say is quite true, and you shall inherit my kingdom." And the King kissed him, and soon after this he died, and the King's son reigned in his stead, and reigned happily ever after as the King of this country.

Once upon a time there was a King and a Queen who had only one daughter, called Windflower. Just before Windflower's ninth birthday, the Queen, her mother, when she was walking in the garden of the palace, found a silver horseshoe lying on one of the paths. Now a silver horseshoe was always found in the garden just before the death of a Queen, so the Queen went to bed at once and sent for her daughter.

"My child," she said, "I have found a silver horseshoe in the garden, and that means I have not long to stay in this world. So listen carefully to what I have to say. You will be the most beautiful Princess the world has ever seen, and I hope you will find a husband who is worthy of you. Take this ring; it is was given to me by my mother, who in her turn received it from my grandmother. The ring is faëry, and you must keep it and wear it always, for as long as you keep it you will be sure of true love; but if you give it away you will give your heart and all its power away with it, and evil will come of this. And if you are blessed with a daughter you must give it to her before you die; but if you have no daughter then you must cast the ring into the sea, for its work will be done."

When the Queen had said this she kissed Windflower and put the ring on her finger. Then she sent for the King and bade him be a good father to their child, and after she had said farewell she fell asleep and never woke up again.

Two years after the Queen died, the King married again. This second wife had already been married before, and she had a daughter of her own who was called Emerald, and who was just the same age as Windflower. As the years rolled on the new Queen became jealous of her step-daughter, because Windflower grew up into the most lovely creature that had ever been seen. She was tall and slender, and her eyes were like dew and her face like the petal of a flower. She danced like the surf of the sea, and she sang like a bird.

But Emerald, although she was handsome, had a proud face, with envious green eyes that glittered balefully. And as, of course, everybody liked Windflower much better than Emerald, this made the Queen angry, and she determined, when the children were grown up and it was time that they should marry, that none of the princes of the land should set eyes on Windflower until Emerald was married. So she sent Windflower to a lonely tower which was in a forest outside the city, and she told the King and the Court that Windflower was not well, and had been ordered by the physicians to live in a quiet place. So Windflower lived by herself in the forest and saw nobody but her old nurse; but she was not sorry to get away from her step-sister, who teased and pinched her dreadfully.

When Emerald's seventeenth birthday came, the King and the Queen prepared a grand banquet to celebrate it, and they invited all the princes of the land, and of these the youngest and the handsomest was Prince Sweetbriar. As he was heir to a large kingdom, the Queen was anxious that he should marry Emerald.

Now it happened that as Prince Sweetbriar was riding to the palace in company with several other Princes, he dropped behind his companions and lost his way, and presently he found himself in the forest where Windflower lived, and he rode past just under the tower. Just then Windflower was leaning out of the window. Her hair, which was like a golden mist, was hanging about her shoulders, and her face blushed like the dawn. Sweetbriar looked up, and he fell in love with her at first sight, and

Windflower looked at him and smiled and fell in love with him too. Then he rode on till he found the city and the palace.

The Queen paid every attention to him, and gave him the most gorgeous room in the palace. The banquet was held in the evening, and after it was over there was a State ball. Sweetbriar looked everywhere for Windflower, but in vain. He asked one of the courtiers whether the King had not got another daughter, and he was told that there was another called Windflower, but nobody ever saw her because she was ill. But Sweetbriar could think of nothing else but Windflower's face, and, in spite of all the Queen did, he took no notice of Emerald.

When the ball was over he found out from his page, who had been gossiping in the kitchen, that Windflower was none other than the beautiful maiden he had seen in the forest. So early next morning he set out for the forest, and he found the tower without difficulty. Windflower looked even more beautiful than before, and Sweetbriar declared his love and asked her to be his wife, and she answered "Yes," and they spent the whole morning together, talking about how happy they would be.

Then Sweetbriar rode back to the palace and asked the King for the hand of his daughter Windflower, whom he had met in the forest. The Queen, of course, tried to make objections, but Sweetbriar would not hear of them; so the King gave his consent, and the Queen could do nothing more, and Sweetbriar and Windflower were married.

For a year they were as happy as the day is long, and a little daughter was born to them whom they christened Sundew; but after a year had gone by the Queen took counsel with her daughter Emerald, and said—

"All is not yet lost, and if you are skilful we may defeat the minx yet. You have only to persuade Sweetbriar to make Windflower give him the ring which her mother gave to her, and all will be well."

"I will do it," said Emerald.

So one day Emerald said to Sweetbriar: "You have a very beautiful wife. I hope she is as devoted as she is beautiful."

"Of course she is!" said Sweetbriar.

"Do you think she would do anything you wished?" asked Emerald.

"Of course," answered Sweetbriar.

Then Emerald laughed, and said: "I am sure she would not even give you the ring she wears on her finger."

Sweetbriar laughed, but Emerald only said: "Try."

So that very same day Sweetbriar said to Windflower: "Emerald is so jealous of you that she says you would not even give me the ring which you wear on your finger, if I ask it of you."

Windflower was distressed when she heard this, and she told Sweetbriar of her mother's warning, and Sweetbriar said that she had much better not give him the ring, since he needed no ring to tell him that she loved him.

But when he next saw Emerald she mocked him, and said: "What did I tell you? She doesn't even love you enough to give you a ring!" And every day Emerald taunted him like this, and she said: "I've no doubt she finds excellent excuses, but she will never give you the ring!"

At last one day Sweetbriar could bear it no longer, and he said to Windflower: "What does it matter if you give your heart away to me? Your heart belongs to me already, so there can be no harm in giving me the ring. Give it to me, for I can no longer bear Emerald's taunts."

So Windflower gave him the ring. Now the ring, as I said, was faëry; as long as she kept it her heart was her own and had the power to bind her husband's heart, but as soon as she gave the ring away, she gave away her heart and with it all its power; so that, although her heart still belonged to Sweetbriar, Sweetbriar's love no more belonged to her—and he soon forgot all about Windflower.

As soon as the Queen and Emerald saw this, they drove Windflower and her child from the palace, and left them in a wood to perish, and they said they had been devoured by wild beasts, and Sweetbriar was wedded to Emerald.

But Windflower and Sundew did not perish. A woodcutter showed them the way out of the wood, and they wandered for several years from city to city begging their bread. One day, when they were both very hungry, and Windflower had just earned a crust of bread, an old woman came up to her and asked for alms.

"I have got no money," said Windflower, "but take this; you need it more than we do." And she gave her the crust of bread.

"You are a good child," said the old woman; "keep your bread and ask for a gift and I will give it you."

"The only gift I crave is what nobody can give," said Windflower. "It is my husband's love, which has been taken from me." And she told the old woman her story.

And the old woman said: "There is only one way of winning back your husband's love. You must earn the ring which you gave him, and he must give it you back and your heart with it in return for his life." So saying the old woman disappeared.

Windflower at once set out for the King's city, and when she got there she found every one in woe and trouble because Prince Sweetbriar was lying mortally sick and nobody could cure him. The King had offered half his kingdom to any one who should cure the Prince, but nobody had even tried.

Windflower, who was in rags and quite unrecognisable, crept into the kitchen and begged a little bread for herself and her little daughter Sundew. She was allowed to warm herself at the fire, and she heard that the Prince had been wounded by a poisoned arrow, and that if some one would suck the poison from his wound he would recover; but nobody would do this, for they knew that they would die themselves, and what was the use of half a kingdom to a dead man?

So Windflower went to the King, and offered to cure the Prince on the condition that he should give her as a gift anything she should ask for.

The King agreed, and Windflower went to the Prince and sucked the poison from his arm. Sweetbriar at once began to get well, and he asked Windflower what she craved as a reward.

"The ring upon your finger," said Windflower.

Sweetbriar gave her the ring, and immediately her heart came back to her, and with it Sweetbriar's love, and he remembered everything and recognised Windflower, and with a great cry he took her in his arms.

And Windflower's heart overflowed with joy. She slipped the ring on her little daughter's finger, then she looked at her husband and smiled, and fell asleep in his arms. She never woke up again, because the poison she had sucked from Sweetbriar's wound was deadly.

And Sweetbriar drove Emerald and her mother from the house, and although his heart was broken, he said no word and he shed no tear, for he knew that it had all come about through his own fault, and that Windflower was very happy and glad to be asleep, because she was so tired.

But his little daughter Sundew laughed, and played with him every day, and she mended his broken heart for him very well, although it was never quite the same as it had been before. And she grew up to be as beautiful and as good as Windflower, and she never gave away her mother's ring.

THE MERCHANT'S DAUGHTER

(A GREEK STORY)

Once upon a time, long ago in Greece, there was a merchant, who used to earn his living by trafficking with goods among the Greek Islands and along the coast of Asia. Sometimes he used to go as far as Persia and India. He possessed many argosies, and he used to take with him large bales of embroideries, silks and other stuffs, spikenard, and all kinds of rare scents and ointments, and these he used to sell for as much money as he could get for them.

But although he was wealthy, he was a kind merchant; and although he considered trade to be important, and struck as good a bargain as he could, when the time for bargaining came, yet there was something that he considered more important than merchandise and than bargaining, and that was his daughters. He had three daughters. The eldest was called Heliodore, the second Hermione, and the third Daphne. They were all three of them extremely beautiful. The eldest, Heliodore, was tall like a lily; the second, Hermione, was dark like a rose; and the third, Daphne, was like a flower that grows in the springtime.

One day, when his daughters were grown up, it was necessary for the merchant to make a long journey to the East—a longer journey than he had ever made before. He was obliged to go to India in order to sell some vases cunningly worked, which Indian princes were especially fond of. Before he started he called his daughters to him and said good-bye to them. They each of them kissed him on both cheeks, and begged him to bring them back something from India. They knew that India was a marvellous country, full of rich and strange things. He promised to bring back something for each of them, and he asked them what they would like. Heliodore said she would like a scarf woven of moonbeams, such as is only to be found in the mountains which are in the north of India. Hermione said she would like a necklace made of rubies, such as are only found in the mines of India, where little gnomes work all day and all night underground and never see the sky. But when he asked Daphne what she would like, she answered: "The only thing that I want is the Golden Ring." And Heliodore and Hermione laughed at her, and said: "Silly child! she could buy a golden ring in any shop in Athens. What a foolish thing to ask for."

Before the merchant started, Heliodore, Hermione, and Daphne burnt a sacrifice on the altar of Hermes, and they prayed that the winds and the waves might be favourable to their father, and they entreated him that he should remember his promise to them, and should not forget the gifts which they desired; and they said at the end of their prayer: "If our father forgets to bring back these gifts which he has promised us, then grant us that his ship, swift Hermes, may not stir from the shore." And the merchant confirmed their prayer, and burnt incense on the altar himself. Then he started for India.

He arrived in India without difficulty, and during several months he carried on his trade and did excellent business. He sold cunningly wrought cups to the Indian princes, and statues, and garments, and sandals, and lamps, and many other things besides. He travelled all over India, trafficking and striking bargains; and during his travels he went up to the northern mountains, and bought from an old woman a veil made of moonbeams, for his eldest daughter Heliodore. This veil was expensive, and he was obliged to give in exchange for it some of the grass of Parnassus, gathered while Apollo was playing upon his fiddle, and some water from the spring of Helicon, taken in a crystal flask on the night when the Muses cease from quarrelling and sing in unison to the new moon.

After he had bought this veil at such a high price, he went to the plains in the centre of India, and walked into the heart of a mountain, and reached the caves which are under the earth, where the gnomes work all day and all night, and there he asked the King of the Gnomes to sell him the necklace of rubies. The King of the Gnomes said: "What will you give me for it?" And the merchant said: "I will give you whatever you ask." And the King of the Gnomes said to him: "I will have in exchange for a necklace of rubies the nightingale that sings in the thickets of Daulis." So the merchant gave him this nightingale, although he was sorry to part with it, and received the necklace of rubies in exchange.

The merchant remembered these gifts, which were so difficult to get, but he quite forgot what he had promised to his third daughter, which was only a golden ring, and he started home without the golden ring. When he reached the coast, and embarked on his argosy, there was a fair breeze, and he was pleased because he thought his journey would be swift. But what was his surprise to find that the ship would not stir from the shore. Many other ships belonging to other sailors were scudding fast through the waves, leaving behind them a trail of foam, and yet his ship, although she was an excellent seaboat, refused to stir. And this lasted all day and all night.

At last he disembarked and sat down on the shore, and thought, saying to himself, "What spell has been put on my ship? What have I done? In what way have I displeased the gods that they prevent me from going home?"

As he was pondering over this, a peasant walked along the coast. He was carrying a basket of eggs home from the market, and he stopped and asked the merchant what he was thinking of.

The merchant hardly liked to tell him about his private family affairs, but the peasant said to him: "I am sure there is something on your mind, otherwise it is impossible that your ship should not be scudding over the sea. Perhaps you promised something to somebody before you started."

The merchant thought about this, and then at last he remembered what he had promised to Daphne, and he said to the peasant: "I promised my daughter to bring her back the Golden Ring from India, and I have forgotten to do so."

The peasant said: "That accounts for it all. If you have promised to bring back something to somebody who is dear to you and have forgotten it, it is quite impossible that you should sail back home."

"That is all very well," said the merchant, "but can you tell me where I can find the Golden Ring? You see, there are many golden rings everywhere, but my daughter Daphne, who is my youngest daughter, asked me to bring her back the Golden Ring."

The peasant nodded and turned round, and then he said: "You see this road running in front of you into the distance? Walk along it, without looking to the right or to the left, and when you have walked for three hours you will reach a spot, and in that spot is the Golden Ring."

The merchant did what the peasant had told him, and he walked for three hours without looking to the right or to the left. When the three hours were over he reached a milestone, on which was written: "To the Coast, three hours; to the Palace, one minute." Near the milestone an old man with a long grey beard was sitting, so the merchant spoke to the old man, and said to him: "Sir, can you tell me where I can find the Golden Ring?"

The old man answered him: "The Golden Ring is in the palace of the King. The palace of the King is a minute's walk from here. You turn to the right, and before you you will find two golden gates. You must open these gates, walk through them, and you will find the palace of the King in front of you. In this palace there is a Prince, who is the King's son, and that Prince is the Golden Ring."

The merchant did as he was told. He walked for a minute, and found in front of him two golden gates. Here he stopped a moment, because he was afraid to walk into the house of somebody whom he did not know. Nevertheless he took heart and opened the gates, and walked straight along a broad road until he reached the steps which led to the front door of the King's palace. Now the King's palace was made entirely of red marble, and when the merchant saw it he was frightened. However, he walked up the steps, and knocked loudly on the door, and immediately a slave appeared and asked him what he wanted.

"I wish to see the King," said the merchant, "and to ask him if I may enter into his palace."

The slave went away, and presently he came back again and said to the merchant: "The King will be very glad if you will do him the honour of entering his palace. Moreover, the King would like to talk to you himself. He is at this moment in the Throne Room, sitting on the throne."

So the merchant was ushered into the Throne Room, and there was the King sitting on a throne made of ivory and studded with emeralds. As he entered this room, the King walked down the steps of the throne, and asked him politely what was his business.

The merchant said: "Your Majesty, I want to speak to the Prince."

The King said that nothing was easier, and he led the merchant through a long corridor into another room, which belonged to the Prince.

The Prince was a young man, scarcely twenty-one years old. His hair was as bright as the rice-fields in winter, and his eyes were as blue as the sea. He was strong and nimble, and his voice was as tuneful as a bell.

The Prince said to the merchant: "I am very glad to see you. I am always glad to see people who come from a far country; but what do you want of me?"

So the merchant told him all his story—how he had three daughters; how he had remembered to bring back the gifts which the two eldest had asked of him; and how he had forgotten the Golden Ring which he had promised to his youngest daughter, Daphne.

Then the Prince said: "I quite understand. Is your daughter Daphne very beautiful?"

And the merchant said: "All my daughters are beautiful. My eldest daughter, Heliodore, is as beautiful as the day; and my second daughter, Hermione, is as glorious as the night; but my third daughter, Daphne, is like the first day of spring. She is more beautiful than any woman in the world."

Then the Prince led him along a long corridor into a room in which there were many beautiful pictures of beautiful women; and he said to the merchant: "Is your daughter Daphne as beautiful as any of the people who are pictured here?"

And the merchant said: "My daughter Daphne is a thousand times more beautiful than any of these pictures."

And the Prince knew by the tone of voice in which he said it, that what he said was true. He then led him into another room, in which there was only one picture, and this was a picture of a woman he had once seen long ago, in a dream, when he had dreamt of her who should be his wife; and this picture was the most beautiful picture in the world; and the woman who was painted in this picture was like a dream or a vision, so that those people who looked at it could not believe that such a beautiful thing could possibly be true. When the Prince had drawn the curtain from this picture he said to the merchant, "Is your daughter as beautiful as that?" and the merchant answered, "That is my daughter Daphne." Then the Prince said to him: "I thought so. I will give you something to take back to her."

He took the merchant into another room, and gave him a letter written on parchment, a cup made of crystal, and a small golden ring of plain gold, and he said to the merchant: "Please do not forget to take these three gifts to your youngest daughter, Daphne. Farewell."

The Prince said good-bye to the merchant, and the King said good-bye to him also, and a slave was sent with him to show him the way out of the palace, and the nearest road to the coast; and there he found his ship waiting for him, and directly he got on board and set sail, the ship answered to the breeze, and swiftly and surely he arrived in his native country.

Now no sooner had he got home than his daughters asked him: "Father, have you brought us back the presents which you promised us?"

"Yes," said the merchant, "I have. I have brought Heliodore a veil woven of moonbeams, which I found in the northern hills of India, and it was very expensive. And I have brought Hermione a necklace of rubies, in exchange for which I had to part with a precious nightingale. And I have brought Daphne the gifts which she asked for." So saying, he gave his daughters their various presents, and to Daphne the letter, the cup, and the ring which the Prince had given him.

When Heliodore and Hermione saw what their father had brought Daphne, they were very pleased, because they thought a piece of paper, a cup such as was to be seen in almost any shop in Athens, and a golden ring worth at the most a few pieces of silver, were indeed shabby presents compared with the treasures which they had received, and they laughed at their sister.

But Daphne paid no heed to this. She took her gifts to her room, and locked herself in, and there she unrolled the scroll of paper which her father had given her, and read what was written in it. It was written on the parchment that she was to pour water into the crystal cup, throw the Golden Ring into it, and call three times aloud: "Come hither, come hither, come hither, my Golden Ring!" No sooner had she read this than she filled the crystal cup with water, threw the Golden Ring into it, and called out to the ring as she had been told to do; and as she called, lo and behold! a wood-pigeon flew into her room and alighted on the crystal cup, and dived and swam in the water; and as soon as its body was completely immersed in the water, it changed into the very Prince whom the merchant had seen in India.

"I am Prince Fortunate," said the Prince, "and I live in India. I have seen you many times in my dreams, and the first time I saw you I made up my mind that you should be my wife, for you are the most beautiful woman in the world, and I love you with all my heart." And Daphne told the Prince that she loved him too, although she had never seen him before, except in her dreams, and they talked happily together for more than an hour.

Then the Prince dipped his fingers into the crystal cup, and instantly changed into a wood-pigeon, and flew away through the window. But before he flew away, the bird gave Daphne a nut, and told her to crack it and to put on what she should find inside it.

As soon as Daphne was left alone, she cracked the nut, and she found inside it a beautiful dress, as dark as a summer night, but on the folds of which were painted the sun, the moon, and all the stars of heaven. She put it on, and went for a walk in the garden, and her dress shone like a starry night, and it was a wonderful sight to behold; and her sisters, who were leaning out of a window which overlooked the garden, were dazzled by the sight of the shining garment, and they wondered greatly, and they were filled with envy and jealousy.

The next day all this happened again. The pigeon flew in at Daphne's window, changed into the Prince, and talked to her for an hour, and when the hour was over changed back into a pigeon again and flew away, leaving her a fig, which he told her to cut open, and to wear what she should find inside it. She cut open the fig, and inside it she found a dress on which the azure sea and all its white waves were painted. This dress was like the sea at dawn, when the wind ruffles it, and little waves of crested foam dance for joy in the morning air.

Daphne put it on, and went for a walk in her garden, and her sisters, who were leaning out of the window, were amazed at the lovely sight, and cried out in surprise—for at first they thought it was Queen Aphrodite just fresh from the sea; and they envied Daphne sorely.

The next day the same thing happened again. Daphne threw the ring into the cup, and all happened as before; and when the pigeon flew away, he left her a hazel-nut, and told her to crack it and wear what she should find inside it.

Daphne cracked the hazel-nut, and inside it she found a garment on which the month of May with all its flowers was painted. She put it on, and she again went for a walk in the garden, and her sisters, who were leaning out of the window, gave a great cry when they saw her—for beautiful as had been the dress on which the sun, the moon, and the stars were painted, and beautiful the dress on which were pictured the sea and all its waves, this one was far lovelier still, for it was as frail as blossom, and as soft, and fragrant exceedingly; and as Daphne walked across the grass in it, her sisters thought that Queen Proserpine had left her dismal home and had come back to visit the earth once more, arrayed in the glory of May—and then they saw that it was only their sister Daphne, whom they had always despised. This made Heliodore and Hermione so jealous that they took counsel one with the other how they might do Daphne harm, and at last they settled on a plan.

Every morning, as soon as the sun rose, the three sisters used to go to the baths and bathe. So the morning after Daphne had walked about in the garden, in the dress, on which the month of May and all its flowers were painted, as they were walking together to the baths, Heliodore took with her a bag full of seed-pearls, and all at once she pretended to slip, and in slipping scattered the pearls on to the path. Then she said to Hermione and Daphne, "You go on in front, whilst I pick up my pearls." As soon as Hermione and Daphne were out of sight, she swept up the pearls with a small broom and put them all back into the bag, and then she returned to the house. There she took the key of Daphne's room—for she had noticed that Daphne always hid this key in a crevice on the hearth—and she opened Daphne's door, went into her room, and searched in every corner to see what she might find; and there, at the back of the cupboard, she found the Prince's letter, the crystal cup, and the Golden Ring. She read the Prince's letter, filled the crystal cup with water, threw the Golden Ring into it, and called out the magic words. But it so happened that Daphne had that day left her knife in the cup; so when Heliodore cried out, "Come hither, come hither, come hither, my Golden Ring!" the wood-pigeon flew in at the window, and dived into the crystal cup, but just as he was going to change into the Prince he fell upon the knife, and he flew away with a wound in his breast.

Now when Heliodore saw that there was a drop of blood in the crystal cup, she was afraid, and she ran away from Daphne's room, and rejoined her sisters at the baths.

When they came back from the baths, Daphne went to her room and took the cup from the cupboard. But when she saw that there was a drop of blood in it, she cried bitterly, for she saw what had happened, and she understood what her sister had done; and when she had cried for a long time by herself, she went out of doors, and she found her father and said to him: "Oh sir, buy me a man's dress, such as will prevent those who see me from recognising me, when I wear it; and buy me a swift ship, so that I may travel."

Her father gave her the dress and the ship, and she embarked on it and started for India, disguised as a pedlar, in order to find the Prince.

She sailed to India, but when she disembarked, she was at a loss as to what to do, for she did not know where the Prince lived, nor the way to his palace. As she was brooding in her perplexity, she caught sight of two pigeons who were quarrelling with each other, and one of them was threatening to kill the other. Daphne listened to their conversation, for she understood the language of birds because of the Golden Ring which she wore on her finger. And one of the birds was saying to the other: "Prince Fortunate is sick, and the physicians do not know how to cure him." And the other bird said: "Will he be cured?" And the first pigeon answered: "If some one were to kill us and to dip our bodies in the spring which is hard by, and then make an ointment of the water of the spring, and rub the Prince with that ointment, he would surely get well."

Directly Daphne heard this she took a stone and killed the pigeons, and dipped them into the water of the spring, and made an ointment, as they had said. No sooner had she done this than a wandering minstrel passed her, and asked her whither she was going.

"I am looking," said Daphne, "for the King's palace, where Prince Fortunate lives, but I do not know where it is."

The minstrel said: "Come with me, for I know the way. But what is your trade?"

"I am a physician," said Daphne, "and I have good medicine to sell."

So presently she reached the King's palace, and called outside the windows: "Good medicine to sell. Good medicine to sell."

When the King heard that there was a physician there, he sent for him and said: "Can you cure my son?"

Daphne answered: "In eight days I will make him so well that he will ride on his horse, and shoot with his bow and arrow."

The King was pleased; but when the other doctors heard of this, they said that if this new physician cured the King's son in a week, the King would be at liberty to cut off their heads.

So Daphne, in the disguise of a doctor, was taken to the Prince, and she rubbed him with the ointment she had made, and instantly he grew a little better, and in two or three days' time he grew much better, and in a week's time he was quite well and able to ride on his horse and to shoot with his bow and arrow.

Now, when the King saw this, he was greatly pleased, and he said to the physician: "You have cured my son; what can I do for you in return?"

And the physician answered, "All I desire is that your Majesty should give a great banquet, and invite to it all the kings and princes of India."

The King said: "That is but a trifling favour to ask." And he gave orders at once that a great feast should be prepared, and he invited to it all the kings and princes of India, Persia, and Arabia, and they ate and drank and made merry.

When the banquet was over, Daphne, in the disguise of the doctor, said to the King: "Let there be silence, for I have a story to tell the company." The King gave orders, and every one was silent. Then Daphne told the whole of her story, as I have told it now, and she told everything except one thing—she did not say who she was, for she was keeping this to the end. But when she reached the end of the story and told how the merchant's daughter had disguised herself as a doctor in order to cure the Prince, she said—

"I am the merchant's daughter. My name is Daphne, and in the disguise of a doctor I cured the Prince. I did it because I am betrothed to him, and because he will make me his wife; and I never did the Prince any harm, but my sister did that evil thing from envy, because she was jealous of our happiness."

As soon as the Prince heard this, he recognised Daphne, and he embraced her and said: "It is true. This is Daphne, my betrothed, and my bride that is to be."

And the King prepared a splendid wedding-feast, which lasted three days, and they were married in a temple of gold, and on the first day of the feast Daphne wore the dress on which the sun, the moon, and the stars were painted; and on the second day she wore the dress on which were pictured the sea and all its waves; but on the third day she wore the dress which was adorned with the month of May and all its flowers, and on that day she was more beautiful than ever she had been before, for it was her wedding-day. And she lived with the Prince happily for ever afterwards.

THE CUNNING APPRENTICE

(A RUSSIAN STORY)

Once upon a time there was an old man and an old woman who had one son. The old man was poor, and he wished his son to acquire knowledge, so that he should be able to comfort his parents in his youth, to support them when he grew up, and to pray for them after their death. But what is to be done when one has no money? He took him to the village. "Perhaps," he thought, "somebody will give him lessons for nothing." But nobody wished to teach his son for nothing. The old man returned home, and he and his wife cried bitterly, lamenting their poverty.

Once more he took his son to the town. As soon as he reached the town a stranger met them, and asked what was the matter. "Why, old man," he said, "are you so sad?"

"How can I not be sad?" answered the old man. "Look, I have taken my son everywhere, and nobody will teach him for nothing, and I have no money."

"Well, give him to me," said the stranger, "and in three years I will teach him all the knowledge there is. And in three years' time, on this same day and at the same hour, come and fetch your son. But take care that you are not late, for if you come in time and recognise him you shall receive your son back again, but if you are late he shall remain with me."

The old man was so pleased that he did not ask who the stranger was, where he lived, or how and what he would teach the lad. He left his son with him, and went home. He reached home in great joy, and told his wife all about it. Now the stranger was a wizard.

Three years passed. The old man had long ago forgotten on what day and at what hour he had left his son with the stranger, and he did not know what to do. But the son, on the day before the appointed space of time came to an end, flew to him in the shape of a bird, and entered the cottage in his true shape. He greeted his parents, and said: "Father, to-morrow my apprenticeship, which has lasted three years, comes to an end. Do not forget to come and fetch me." And he told him where to come and how to recognise him.

"I am not the only apprentice at my master's: there are eleven more lads like myself, who remain with him for ever, and all because their parents did not know how to recognise them. And if you do not recognise me, I shall also stay with him for ever, and be the twelfth. To-morrow, when you come for me, my master will change us into twelve white pigeons, all alike, feather for feather, tail for tail, and head for head. Now listen: All of us will fly high in the air, but I will fly higher than the rest. My master will ask, 'Have you recognised your son?' And you must then point to the pigeon which is flying higher than the others. After this he will bring to you twelve ponies, all of the same colour, and all with their manes on the same side, and just alike. When he takes you to these ponies they will all be standing still, but I shall give a kick with my right leg. My master will ask you, 'Have you recognised your son?' And you must then point me out. After this he will bring to you twelve lads, all of the same height, all alike, hair for hair and voice for voice, and all dressed alike. As soon as you see them look carefully; on my right cheek there will be a little fly, so that you may recognise me."

He said good-bye to his parents, and went out of the house, changed into a bird and flew away to his master.

The next morning his father got up, made ready and went to fetch his son. He arrived at the wizard's. "Now, old man," said the wizard, "I have taught your son everything that is to be known, but if you don't recognise him, he must stay with me for ever and ever." He then let fly into the air twelve white pigeons, all alike, feather for feather, tail for tail, and head for head; and he said: "Old man, do you recognise your son?"

The old man looked and looked, and when one pigeon flew higher than the rest, he pointed to it and said: "I think that is my son."

"You have recognised him, old man," said the wizard. He then brought twelve ponies, all of the same colour, and their manes all on the same side. The old man walked round the ponies and looked, and the wizard asked: "Now, old man, have you recognised your son?" "Not yet, wait a little." And when he said that, one of the ponies gave a kick with his right leg. He pointed to him immediately and said: "I think that is my son."

"You have recognised him, old man," said the wizard. He then brought him to twelve lads, all of the same height, all alike, hair for hair, and voice for voice, as if they were the children of one mother. The old man walked round the lads and noticed nothing. He did so a second time, and again noticed nothing. He walked round them a third time, and then he saw that on the right cheek of one of the lads there was a fly, and he said: "I think that is my son."

"You have recognised him, old man. Yes, and it is not you who are cunning and wise, but it is your son."

The old man took his son and went home. They walked along the road, and whether it was long or whether it was short, and whether it was far or whether it was near, it takes but little time to tell, but it took a long time to do. On their way they met some huntsmen who were hunting a red beast. In front of them a fox was running as though it would escape.

"Father," said the son, "I will turn myself into a hound and catch the fox. When the huntsmen come up to take the animal, say to them, 'O! huntsmen, that is my dog; I make my living by him.' The huntsmen will say, 'Sell him to us,' and they will count out to you much money. Sell the dog, but do not give them the collar and the chain." He immediately changed himself into a hound, ran after the fox and caught it. The huntsmen rode up. "Old man," they cried, "why have you come here to spoil our hunt?"

"O! huntsmen," answered the old man, "that is my dog; I make my living by him."

"Sell him to us."

"Buy it."

"Is it dear?"

"A hundred roubles."

The huntsmen did not bargain, but paid him the money and took the dog, and the old man took off its collar and its chain. "Why do you take off the collar and the chain?"

"I am a traveller," said the old man, "and the chain is necessary to me to bind up my cloth leggings."

"All right, take it," said the huntsmen, and they whipped their horses and rode off at a gallop. But the fox got away again; they started their hounds after it; the hounds ran but could not catch the fox. One of the huntsmen said: "Let us try the new hound." They let it loose, and what did they see? The fox ran off in one direction, and the hound in another, and he caught up the old man and changed into a lad just as he had been before.

The old man went on further with his son. They came to a lake where huntsmen were shooting geese, swans, and wild ducks. A flock of geese was flying, and the son said to his father: "Father, I will change myself into a hawk, and I will pursue the geese. The huntsmen will come to you and begin to make a fuss. You say to them, 'That is my hawk; I make my living by him.' They will bargain with you for the hawk. You sell the hawk, but do not give up its jesses on any account." He changed himself into a hawk, flew higher than the flock of geese, and began pursuing them and driving them to the earth. As soon as the huntsmen saw this, they came to the old man and said: "Old man, why are you spoiling our sport?"

"O! huntsmen," he answered, "the hawk is mine, and I earn my living by him."

"Will you sell your hawk?"

"Why should I not sell him? Buy him."

"And is it dear?"

"Two hundred roubles."

The huntsmen paid the money, took the hawk, and the old man took off its jesses. "Why are you taking off the jesses?"

"I am a traveller," answered the old man, "and if something comes off my leggings, they serve to tie them up with." The huntsmen did not dispute the matter, but went after their game. The flock of geese flew away. "Let us loose the hawk," they said, and they loosed him, but what did they see? The hawk flew higher than the geese, and flew right away to the old man, and caught him up, touched the green ground, and changed himself back into a lad as he had been before. And the father and son went home and lived in clover.

Sunday came, and the son said to his father: "Father, to-day I will change myself into a horse. You shall sell the horse, but on no account sell the bridle, for if you do I shall not come home again." He rolled on the earth and changed into a magnificent horse, and his father led him off to sell him. The merchants surrounded him, horse-dealers all of them; one of them offered a large sum of money, another offered a still larger sum of money. But the wizard, who appeared there, offered more than all of them. The old man sold him his son, but did not give him the bridle.

"And how shall I be able to lead the horse without a bridle?" said the wizard. "Give me the bridle to lead him as far as my house, and then take it back, for I do not want it."

Then the horse-dealers fell upon the old man and said: "That is only fair; if you sell the horse you must sell the bridle." What could he do? The old man gave up the bridle. The wizard led the horse to his house, put it in the stables, tied it fast to the ring, and pulled his head up high so that the horse stood on his hind legs, and his fore legs did not touch the ground. The wizard called his daughter and said: "I have bought the cunning fellow." "Where is he?" asked his daughter. "He is in the stables." His daughter went to see, and she was sorry for the young lad. She loosened the bridle and made it longer, and the horse shook his head so that at last he freed himself from the bridle, and galloped away for several miles. The daughter ran to her father and said: "Father, forgive me, I have done a wicked thing. The horse has escaped."

The wizard struck the green earth, changed himself into a grey wolf, and pursued the horse. As soon as he got near him the horse galloped to a river, struck the earth and changed himself into a minnow, and the wizard changed himself into a pike. The minnow scudded through the water and reached a pond, where beautiful maidens were washing linen and wringing it out. He changed himself into a golden ring and lay close by the hand of the merchant's daughter. The merchant's daughter saw the ring and put it on her finger. The wizard changed himself into a man once more, and said: "Give me your golden ring."

"Take it," said the beautiful maiden, and threw the ring on to the ground. As soon as it struck the ground, in that moment it changed into a seed-pearl. The wizard changed himself into a cock and ran to pick up the seed-pearl. But before he had picked it up, the pearl changed into a hawk, and the hawk immediately flew at the cock, and killed him. After that he changed once more into a fine lad, and fell in love with the beautiful maiden, the daughter of the merchant, and married her. And they lived happily and merrily together.

That is the end of the story.

(A GREEK STORY)

There was once upon a time a King who had three sons and one daughter. Not far from the King's palace there was a large garden, and in this garden lived a dragon. The King told his children never to go into the garden lest they should be caught by the dragon, which had wings. But one evening the youngest of the King's sons, whose name was Orestes, went with his sister into the garden and began to play. No sooner had they begun to play than the dragon appeared, and seizing the little Princess with its tail, flew away into the air and took her to a high mountain which no one could climb.

When Orestes went home and told of the misfortune, the King was very sad, and a black flag was hoisted on the top of the palace, and the whole Court went into mourning.

Now Orestes, since it had been through his fault that his sister had been lost, wished to be allowed to seek her; but his father would not let him do this, for Orestes was his favourite son. But one day when his father was busy, Orestes stole out of the house and walked to the foot of the high mountain, whither the dragon had taken his little sister. He wondered how he could climb it, and the task seemed difficult, indeed almost impossible, since the mountain was as smooth as glass.

While he was thus wondering he noticed two snakes which were fighting. One was black, and the other was white, and the black snake was getting the best of the fight and on the verge of killing the white one. Orestes at once killed the black snake, upon which the white snake said to him—

"You have saved my life! What can I do for you in return?"

"I wish for nothing," said Orestes, "save to be able to climb to the top of this mountain."

"Catch hold of my tail," said the snake, "and I will take you to the top of the mountain."

And the snake wriggled up the mountain, pulling the Prince after him, and as soon as they reached the top it disappeared.

Upon the top of the mountain, Orestes found a shepherd looking after the sheep of the dragon, and he entered into the service of this shepherd as a herdsman. One day when he was looking after the sheep he met his sister, and said to her: "I am your brother Orestes, and I have come to set you free."

His sister was surprised to see him, and frightened, and she said: "We must be very careful and cunning, lest the dragon should find us out, for it is impossible to escape from this place, nor can we save ourselves from the dragon. His rooms are all full of princesses whom he has taken captive, and who cannot climb down the mountain."

And she asked her brother how he had been able to climb it. He told her about the snake, and then he said—

"This evening, when the dragon comes back to his house, ask him where his strength lies, and I will come to-morrow and you shall tell me."

In the evening the dragon came home, and the Princess asked him where his strength lay, and the dragon told her that he had three golden hairs on the top of his head, and with these hairs one could open a room in which there were three doves; and were any one to kill the first dove, he would grow sick; and were any one to kill the second dove, he would grow worse; and if any one were to kill the third dove, he would die.

The next day, when the dragon had gone out on his daily business, which was to look for disobedient children in the country round and to catch them, the Princess went to her brother and told him what the dragon had said.

Orestes told her that when the dragon came back in the evening and fell asleep, she was to take a pair of scissors and cut off the three golden hairs, and open the secret room and kill the doves which were in it.

In the evening when the dragon came back and fell asleep, which he did at once, for he was tired, the Princess took a pair of scissors, cut off his three golden hairs, opened the secret room and killed the doves; and immediately the dragon gave a great groan and died.

As soon as he was dead, all the doors of all the rooms in the house, which had been carefully locked, flew open, and hundreds and hundreds of prisoners were set free. Among these there were three princesses. Orestes and his sister walked with these three princesses to the edge of the mountain top, and when they reached it Orestes saw his brothers, who were waiting at the foot of the hill.

Orestes took a rope, and first he let down his sister; then he let down the eldest of the princesses and said: "She shall be the wife of my eldest brother." Afterwards he let down the second of the princesses, and said: "She shall be the wife of my second brother." And, lastly, he let down the youngest princess, and he said: "This shall be my wife."

But when his brothers saw that the youngest princess was the most beautiful of the three, they were angry, and they jerked the rope out of Orestes' hands and left him on the top of the mountain.

Orestes was most sorrowful, and he went into the castle of the dragon and looked into all the rooms.

Now in one room, which was carpeted with green grass, he found a silken greyhound which was hunting a silken hare; and in another room he found a golden beaker and a golden jug; and in another he found a golden hen with golden chickens. Then he went to the stables, and there in a stall he found three horses with golden wings, and one was white, and one was red, and one was green.

"By opening the doors of our stable," said the horses, "you have done us a great favour. What can we do for you in return?"

"I do not wish for anything," said Orestes, "save to be taken to the foot of this mountain!"

"Get on my back," said the green horse; and Orestes got on his back, and the horse flew in a moment to the bottom of the mountain. Then each of the horses gave him two golden hairs, and said: "When you have need of us, burn one of these hairs and we will come."

After some days had passed, Orestes went into the city where the King, his father, lived, and putting an old blanket over his head he pretended to be a beggar, and entered into the service of a goldsmith.

Now when the little Princess and her two brothers reached their father's house, with the three princesses who had been set free, the King asked them what had become of Orestes, and they said that Orestes had died; and the eldest of the brothers wished to marry the eldest of the princesses, but she refused to wed him unless he could find her the silken greyhound which hunted the silken hare. It was in the house of the dragon.

The King's herald proclaimed this everywhere. Then the beggar said to the goldsmith that he could accomplish the quest. "You need only give me a jug of wine and a basketful of chestnuts, and leave me alone in my room."

The goldsmith did this and shut the beggar up in his room, and he looked through the keyhole to see what he was doing. But the beggar did nothing at all; he merely ate the chestnuts and drank the wine, so the goldsmith went to his bedroom and went to sleep. Then the beggar took one of the hairs which the white horse had given him and burned it, and immediately the white horse appeared and said: "What do you wish?"

"I wish," said the beggar, "that you should bring me the silken greyhound and the silken hare."

The horse brought them immediately, and the beggar gave them to the goldsmith. The goldsmith went to the palace and sold them for much money to the eldest prince.

On Sunday the eldest brother married the eldest princess, and everybody went to a field and played quoits. And the beggar burned another golden hair, and immediately the green horse appeared and brought him a green garment. The beggar put it on, and went into the field and played quoits with the company. After he had played for a whole hour everybody had lost; he alone had won much money, and scattering on the grass the money he had won, he went back to the goldsmith's shop and put the blanket on his head once more.

The next Sunday it was arranged that his second brother should marry the second princess; she said she would not wed him unless he could bring her the golden beaker and the golden jug which were in the house of the dragon.

The King sent for all the goldsmiths in the country, and asked them to get him the golden beaker. And once more the beggar told his master that he could get it, and that all he needed were two basketsful of chestnuts and two jars of wine. And being left alone in a room he ate the nuts and drank the wine. Then he burned one of the hairs, and immediately the red horse appeared, and he said to him: "Bring me the golden beaker and the golden jug."

And the horse brought them, and the beggar went to the King, and the King bought them for a large sum of money. Again they went to play quoits in order to celebrate the second wedding, and the beggar burned another of the hairs, and immediately the red horse came to him and brought him a red garment, and when he put it on he went and played quoits. After he had played for a long time, all had lost save himself, and he went away, leaving the ground strewn with gold coins.

On the following Sunday the youngest princess was to be married to a brother of the King, but she did not wish to wed him, and she said that she would not, unless he brought her the golden hen and the golden chickens.

Once more the beggar obtained these, and on Sunday, when the wedding was to be held, they went and played quoits, and the beggar went riding on a white horse and wearing a white garment; and as he was playing he threw the quoit at his uncle who was to wed the youngest princess, and killed him. And they took him to the palace, and the King said to him: "Why have you killed my brother?"

And the Prince told him everything that had happened, and as soon as the King heard the story he gave orders that the two eldest brothers should be put to death, and he gave the youngest princess to Orestes for a wife.

And they were married, and they lived happily for ever afterwards.

THE WISE PRINCESS

(A RUSSIAN STORY)

Once upon a time in a certain kingdom there lived a King and a Queen. They had three sons, who were all young, unmarried, and so brave that no fairy tale could tell, no pen could write down, how brave they were. The youngest was called Ivan-the-King's-Son. The King spoke to his children thus: "My dear children, take each of you an arrow, draw your bow at a venture, and shoot in various directions. And there, where the arrow shall fall, go take a wife."

The eldest brother drew his bow at a venture, and the arrow fell on a nobleman's house, right opposite the women's attic. The second arrow fell in the yard of a merchant's house, on a flight of steps; and on the steps stood a beautiful girl, the merchant's daughter. The youngest brother drew his bow at a venture, and the arrow fell into a dirty marsh, and a frog caught it.

Ivan-the-King's-Son said: "How can I marry a frog? She is not my size."

"Marry her," said the King. "It means that such is your fate."

So the sons of the King were married. The eldest married the nobleman's daughter; the second one, the merchant's daughter; and Ivan-the-King's-Son married a frog. And the King called them to him and gave the following command:—

"Each of your wives must bake me a soft white loaf of bread for breakfast to-morrow."

Ivan-the-King's-Son went to his room with a heavy heart and hung his head.

"Ivan-the-King's-Son, why are you so sad?" the frog asked. "Has your father spoken an angry or an unkind word to you?"

"How can I not be sad? The King, my father, has ordered you to get ready a loaf of soft white bread for his breakfast to-morrow."

"Do not worry, Ivan-the-King's-Son, go to bed and sleep. In the morning you will be wiser than in the evening."

She sent him to bed, and no sooner had she done so than she threw off her frog's skin and turned into a most beautiful girl, for she was none other than the Wise Princess. She went out on to the steps and called out in a loud voice: "Oh you, my nurses, get ready, get ready! Provide yourselves with what is necessary, and make me a white loaf such as I used to eat in my father's house."

In the morning, when Ivan-the-King's-Son got up, the frog's loaf had been ready for some time, and it was so excellent that the like of it had never been seen. The loaf of bread was ornamented with various devices: on the sides of it were kings' palaces, and stately towers with their gardens and their walls. The King thanked Ivan-the-King's-Son for the loaf, and at the same time he gave the following order to his three sons:—

"Your wives shall each of them weave me a carpet by to-night."

Ivan-the-King's-Son came home with a heavy heart and hung his head.

"Croak, croak," said the frog, "why are you so sad? Has your father spoken a cruel or an unkind word to you?"

"How can I not be sad?" answered Ivan-the-King's-Son. "The King, my father, has ordered a silken carpet to be woven for him by to-night."

"Do not worry, Ivan-the-King's-Son, lie down and sleep. In the morning you will be wiser."

She put him to bed, and threw off her frog's skin, and turned into a beautiful maiden. She went out on to the steps and called out in a loud voice: "Oh, you boisterous winds, bring hither that same carpet on which I used to sit in the house of my father."

No sooner said than done. In the morning, when Ivan-the-King's-Son awoke, the carpet had been ready for some time, and it was so beautiful that the like of it had never been seen before. It was adorned with gold, silver, and cunning devices. The King thanked his son for the carpet, and at the same time he issued a new command, namely, that his sons were to be present, each with his wife, at the grand review.

Ivan-the-King's-Son returned home with a heavy heart and hung his head.

"Croak, croak, Ivan-the-King's-Son," said the frog, "why are you so sad? Have you heard from your father anything cruel or unpleasant?"

"How can I not be sad? The King, my father, has ordered that I should be present at the review with you. And how can I show you to the people?"

"Do not worry, Ivan-the-King's-Son! Go by yourself, and pay your respects to the King. I will follow; and as soon as you hear a noise like thunder, say, 'My little frog is coming hither in a basket.'"

The two elder brothers appeared at the review with their wives, all in beautiful clothes; they stood there and laughed at Ivan-the-King's-Son, and said: "Why have you come here, brother, without your wife? You might have brought her in your pocket. And where did you find such a beautiful lady?"

Suddenly a loud noise like thunder was heard, and the whole palace shook. The guests were frightened to death, and jumped up from their places and did not know what to do. But Ivan-the-King's-Son said: "Do not be afraid, gentlemen, this is my little frog who has come here in a basket."

A golden coach drove up to the palace, drawn by six horses, and out of it came the Wise Princess, so beautiful that it is impossible to describe her. She took Ivan-the-King's-Son by the hand, and led him to the oaken chairs and the spread tables. The guests began to eat and drink, and to make merry. The Wise Princess, as she drank from a glass, let a drop fall on to her left sleeve; and as she ate a piece of roast swan, she hid one of the bones in her right sleeve. The wives of the elder sons noticed this, and did the same. Afterwards, when the Wise Princess was dancing with Ivan-the-King's-Son, she shook her left sleeve, and at once a lake appeared. She shook her right sleeve, and white swans swam about on the lake.

The King and his guests were astonished, and when the elder sons' wives began to dance they shook their left sleeves, but the only result of it was to splash the guests. Then they shook their right sleeves, and in so doing a swan's bone hit the King in the face. The King was angry, and drove them away in disgrace. During that time Ivan-the-King's-Son took the opportunity of going home. He found the frog's skin, and threw it into a big fire.

The Wise Princess arrived and asked where her frog's skin was. Then not finding it, she grew sad and said: "Oh, Ivan-the-King's-Son, Ivan-the-King's-Son, what have you done? If you had waited a moment I would have been yours for ever. But now good-bye. Seek me at the end of the world, in the Kingdom of Nowhere. Wear out three pairs of iron boots."

So saying, she turned herself into a white swan, and flew away out of the window.

Ivan-the-King's-Son wept bitterly, and prayed to God with all his might. He put on iron boots, and walked on straight in front of him. He walked and walked, and after a time he met an old man.

"Good morrow, young man," said the old man; "what are you looking for and where are you going to?"

Ivan-the-King's-Son told him all his misfortunes.

"Ah, Ivan-the-King's-Son, why did you burn the frog's skin? You did not put it on, and it was not for you to take it off. The Wise Princess was so far more cunning and wise than her father, that he clothed her in a frog's skin and bade her be a frog for three years. Here is a ball for you. Wherever it rolls, you must boldly follow."

Ivan-the-King's-Son thanked the old man, and followed where the ball rolled. Whether it rolled far or near, for a short time or a long time, the story does not say; but it stopped at a cottage. This cottage stood on chicken's legs and wobbled about. Ivan-the-King's-Son said—

"Cottage, cottage, stand as you used to stand—still, as your mother placed you, back to the wood and front to me."

The cottage turned round, with its back to the wood and its front to him. Ivan-the-King's-Son went into the cottage, and there lay an old woman, all bony, with a nose which grew to the ceiling. She said to him in an angry voice: "Fie, fie, fie! Why have you come here, Ivan-the-King's-Son?"

"Oh, you old woman," he answered, "before asking me questions you should give me something to eat and to drink, and you should prepare me a hot steam bath; and then you can ask me questions."

The old woman gave him food and drink, and a steam bath, and then the King's son told her he was looking for his wife, the Wise Princess.

"My child," said the old woman, "it is a pity you did not come before. In the first years, after her flight, she remembered you, but now she has ceased thinking of you. Go at once to my second sister; she knows more than I do."

Ivan-the-King's-Son set out on his journey, and followed the ball. He walked and walked, and again there stood before him a cottage with chickens' legs.

"Cottage, cottage, stand still, as your mother placed you, with your back to the wood and your front to me."

The cottage turned round. Ivan-the-King's-Son went into it, and there stood an old woman with bony legs. She saw the Prince and she said: "Fie, fie! Ivan-the-King's Son, have you come here of your own accord or because you were obliged to?"

Ivan-the-King's-Son answered: "I have come here of my own accord, and also because I can't help it. I am looking for the Wise Princess."

"I am sorry for you, Ivan-the-King's-Son. You should have come before. The Wise Princess has quite forgotten you. She wants to marry another husband. At this moment she is living with my eldest sister. Go thither quickly, but remember one thing, that as soon as you have entered the cottage, the Wise Princess will turn into a spindle and my sister will begin to spin golden threads, and to turn her wheel. Mind that you lose no time in taking away the spindle from her and breaking it in two; throw half of it behind you and the other half in front of you. Then the Wise Princess will appear."

Ivan-the-King's-Son set out on his journey. He walked and walked, but whether the way was long, or whether it was short, whether it was near or far, the story doesn't say. He wore out three pairs of iron boots, and at last he reached a cottage with chickens' legs.

"Cottage, cottage, stand still, as your mother placed you, with your front to me, and your back to the wood."

The cottage turned round, the King's Son went into it, and there an old woman all bony was sitting and spinning gold. She took her spindle, shut it up in a cupboard, and locked the door with a key. But Ivan-the-King's-Son managed to snatch the key and to open the cupboard. He took the spindle and broke it in two pieces; he threw one piece behind him and one piece in front of him. At the same moment the Wise Princess appeared before him.

"Ah, Ivan-the-King's-Son, what a long time you have been coming! I had nearly married some one else." Then she took him by the hand, and they sat down on a magic carpet, and flew back to Ivan-the-King's-Son's house.

On the fourth day the carpet stopped at the royal palace. The King met his son with great joy and gave a large feast. When it was over, he appointed Ivan-the-King's-Son to be his heir.

MAURICE BARING – A CONCISE BIBLIOGRAPHY

The Black Prince and Other Poems (1903)
With the Russians in Manchuria (1905)
Forget-me-Not and Lily of the Valley (1905)
Sonnets and Short Poems (1906)
Thoughts on Art and Life (1906)
Russian Essays and Stories (1908)
Orpheus in Mayfair and Other Stories (1909) Short stories
Dead Letters (1910) Satirical collection
The Glass Mender and Other Stories (1910)
The Russian People (1911)
Letters from the Near East (1913)
Lost Diaries (1913) Fictional extracts from diaries of notable people
The Mainsprings of Russia (1914)
Round the World in any Number of Days (1919)
Flying Corps Headquarters 1914-1918 (1920)
Passing By (1921) Novel
The Puppet Show of Memory (1922) Autobiography
Overlooked (1922) Short story
Poems 1914-1919 (1923)
C (1924) Novel
Punch and Judy and Other Essays (1924)
Half a Minute's Silence and Other Stories (1925)
Cat's Cradle (1925) Novel
Daphne Adeane (1926) Novel
Tinker's Leave (1927) Novel
Comfortless Memory (1928) Novel
The Coat Without Seam (1929) Novel
Robert Peckham (1930) historical Novel
In My End is My Beginning (1931) Biographical novel about Mary Stuart
Friday's Business (1932) Novel
Lost Lectures (1932) Imaginary lectures

The Lonely Lady of Dulwich (1934) Novella
Darby and Joan (1935) Novel
Have You Anything to Declare? (1936) Collection of notes and quotes
Collected Poems (1937) Poetry
Maurice Baring: A Postscript by Laura Lovat with Some Letters and Verse (1947)
Dear Animated Bust: Letters to Lady Juliet Duff, France 1915-1918
The Oxford Book Of Russian Verse (1924) Editor

Maurice Baring – A Concise Bibliography

The Black Prince and Other Poems (1903)
With the Russians in Manchuria (1905)
Forget-me-Not and Lily of the Valley (1905)
Sonnets and Short Poems (1906)
Thoughts on Art and Life (1906)
Russian Essays and Stories (1908)
Orpheus in Mayfair and Other Stories (1909) Short stories
Dead Letters (1910) Satirical collection
The Glass Mender and Other Stories (1910)
The Russian People (1911)
Letters from the Near East (1913)
Lost Diaries (1913) Fictional extracts from diaries of notable people
The Mainsprings of Russia (1914)
Round the World in any Number of Days (1919)
Flying Corps Headquarters 1914-1918 (1920)
Passing By (1921) Novel
The Puppet Show of Memory (1922) Autobiography
Overlooked (1922) Short story
Poems 1914-1919 (1923)
C (1924) Novel
Punch and Judy and Other Essays (1924)
Half a Minute's Silence and Other Stories (1925)
Cat's Cradle (1925) Novel
Daphne Adeane (1926) Novel
Tinker's Leave (1927) Novel
Comfortless Memory (1928) Novel
The Coat Without Seam (1929) Novel
Robert Peckham (1930) historical Novel
In My End is My Beginning (1931) Biographical novel about Mary Stuart
Friday's Business (1932) Novel
Lost Lectures (1932) Imaginary lectures
The Lonely Lady of Dulwich (1934) Novella
Darby and Joan (1935) Novel
Have You Anything to Declare? (1936) Collection of notes and quotes
Collected Poems (1937) Poetry
Maurice Baring: A Postscript by Laura Lovat with Some Letters and Verse (1947)

Dear Animated Bust: Letters to Lady Juliet Duff, France 1915-1918
The Oxford Book Of Russian Verse (1924) Editor